"We'll find your baby."

For a moment Rand thought she would cry. Instead, she raised her chin and sat up straight, as if forcing all her willpower into her spine.

Echo was some kind of woman. He hated to think how he'd react to losing a child. One reason he'd never entertained having one.

"What are the chances?" she finally asked.

He opened his mouth to give her an answer, then closed it without saying a word. He didn't know the chances. He didn't know what they were up against.

He laid a hand on hers, tracing her soft skin with a fingertip. He shouldn't be touching her now. He was coming dangerously close to getting personally involved. But somehow he couldn't stop himself.

She needed him. He couldn't turn his back. Even though turning his back was exactly what he should do. For her sake. And for his own.

ANN VOSS PETERSON

CRITICAL EXPOSURE

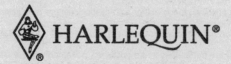

TORONTO • NEW YORK • LONDON
AMSTERDAM • PARIS • SYDNEY • HAMBURG
STOCKHOLM • ATHENS • TOKYO • MILAN • MADRID
PRAGUE • WARSAW • BUDAPEST • AUCKLAND

To my mom, Carol Voss.

And special thanks to Officer Greg Dixon,
Officer David Kasdorf and the Middleton
Police Department for their ideas and assistance.
Any procedural errors, intentional
or otherwise, are mine alone.

ISBN-13: 978-0-373-88726-2
ISBN-10:   0-373-88726-4

CRITICAL EXPOSURE

ABOUT THE AUTHOR

Ever since she was a little girl making her own books out of construction paper, Ann Voss Peterson wanted to write. So when it came time to choose a major at the University of Wisconsin, creative writing was her only choice. Of course, writing wasn't a *practical* choice—one needs to earn a living. So Ann found jobs ranging from proofreading legal transcripts to working with quarter horses to washing windows. But no matter how she earned her paycheck, she continued to write the type of stories that captured her heart and imagination—romantic suspense. Ann lives near Madison, Wisconsin, with her husband, her two young sons, her Border collie and her quarter horse mare. Ann loves to hear from readers. E-mail her at ann@annvosspeterson.com or visit her Web site at annvosspeterson.com.

Books by Ann Voss Peterson

CAST OF CHARACTERS

Randall "Rand" McClellan—A police detective who believes strictly in the evidence, Rand can solve this case only by using his heart.

Echo Sloane—Echo has never found a man she could trust—except for her brother, Bray. So how can she rely on a detective who wants to put her brother in prison? A detective who doesn't even trust his own heart?

Brayden "Bray" Sloane—Echo's brother disappeared after a chemical explosion and hasn't been seen since. Does his vanishing act mean he's in trouble? Or is he to blame?

Wesley Vanderhoven—A victim of the chemical explosion, Wes Vanderhoven has been locked in a psychiatric hospital. But is he there to recover, or is the experimentation continuing?

Dr. Frederick Morton—The man in charge of the Beech Grove psychiatric clinic, Dr. Morton has a lot to hide.

Nurse Dumont—Believing knowledge is power, Nurse Dumont keeps an eye on everything that happens at the Beech Grove clinic.

Ashley Kromm—The nurse is in love with her patient. How far will she go to protect him?

Dr. Martin Kelso—The acting director of Cranesbrook Associates, Kelso is well connected. But is he using those connections for good or evil?

Dr. Nelson Ulrich—The research director cares only about his work. To what lengths is he willing to go to protect it?

Hank Riddell—The research fellow seems to have all the answers at just the right moments.

Chapter One

Officer Maxine Wallace rested her fingers on her weapon's grip. A muscle twitched deep in her throat, steady as a clock's tick. Her nerves trilled with the sense of approaching danger.

Ridiculous.

There was no reason for her to feel so uneasy. As far as the job's duties went, this was a simple task; assist the Maryland State Police by executing a search warrant; gather evidence of whatever crimes the president of chemical-research company Cranesbrook Associates had committed that had caused him to kill people to cover them up.

Not just people, a state police detective.

Determination hardening in her gut, Maxie peered through the office door. She focused on the stain in the anteroom near the glass doors. The cream carpet was still rusty red where Cranesbrook president, Sid Edmonston's, blood had seeped into the fibers and saturated the pad. She could smell it, too. That coppery, fleshy odor only came with blood and death.

She was glad the scumbag himself was in the morgue. She was glad Rand McClellan, Detective Richard Francis's partner, had been the one to fire the shots. It was only right that Rand had delivered justice for his partner's murder. It was right Sid Edmonston would never see a trial. The bastard didn't deserve to live after all he'd done.

The whole mess had started with some kind of lab accident, sending two men to the Beech Grove Clinic mental hospital and leaving one man missing. A lab accident that Sid Edmonston had been desperate to cover up. And if any of Edmonston's files and personal papers contained clues as to *what* he was trying so hard to hide, it was important Maxie get them to the state police barracks as soon as possible.

She pulled her gaze from the bloodstain and shivered. Now that the evidence team had moved to the lab where the accident had occurred, it was quiet in this corner of the administrative wing. Almost too quiet. If she didn't know Officer Woodard was out in the hall securing the scene, she'd believe she was all alone.

She fitted her fingers in the cutout handles of a cardboard file box and hoisted it to her hip. Backing and turning in the tight space, she bumped against the wall. The wall shifted, almost dumping her on the floor.

What in the hell…?

She set the box down and knelt to study the wall. Sure enough, there was a loose panel. She wouldn't have noticed it, not even if she'd been looking. But with the panel skewed where she'd hit it with her hip, she could spot it easily. Pressing her fingertips against a corner, she pried the loose chunk of drywall free.

A small space between the studs hid a thin plastic case. She pulled out a pair of latex gloves. Her fingers trembled at first, making it difficult to get the gloves on her hands. Finally managing, she pulled the DVD case from its hiding spot. Factory lettering marked the face of the disk. A recordable DVD. Lab 7 was scrawled beneath it in black marker. And a date.

The date of the lab accident.

Was this the missing surveillance video from the security cameras in Lab 7? The video that showed what really happened that day?

It had to be.

A surge of adrenaline replaced her unease. If this was what she thought it was, she might have just found what the state needed to put this case to bed. She keyed the microphone on her uniform. "Four two four eight."

"Four two four eight, go ahead."

"I'm at Sid Edmonston's office at

Cranesbrook Associates. I've found what looks like surveillance footage hidden inside a secret compartment in the wall. A detective with the state might want to get out here. Right away."

"Ten-four, four two four eight."

She turned off the mike, not bothering to hide her grin. Why should she? This was a major find. Major enough to possibly win her a commendation. And besides, no one was watching. She could turn cartwheels across the spacious office and no one would know.

The light padding sound of a footfall on carpet came from the anteroom.

Guess she almost cartwheeled too soon.

Still holding the DVD, she stepped from the closet and peered through the inner office's open door.

No one was there.

Funny. She could have sworn she'd heard a sound. Was someone hiding around the corner? Playing some sort of trick? "Woodard? Is that you?"

No answer. No sound.

Wait. There was a sound. A familiar sound, though so out of context it made a chill run down her spine. The light mew of a person crying.

The hair rose on her arms. She rubbed her skin through the long sleeves of her uniform. "Woodard? What the hell are you doing? This is no time to be goofing around."

The sound grew louder, erupting in jagged sobs. Definitely a man.

"Woodard?" She shifted the DVD to her left hand and unsnapped her holster with her right. Taking a deep breath, she forced herself to leave her weapon in its holster. This had to be some sort of practical joke, didn't it? A jab at freaking out the female cop?

It was working.

She shook her head. She didn't freak out easily. Hell, she *never* freaked out. Woodard knew that. If he ever teased her, it was about how inhuman she could be.

So why was he doing this? And why was it frightening her so?

She should walk out into the hall, tell

him to knock it off. But somehow her feet wouldn't move. She opened her mouth. Her voice lodged in her throat.

What was happening to her?

The tremble that had started in her hands moved through her body, seizing her muscles from the inside out. She gritted her teeth, trying to get a grip. She felt so frightened. No, not merely frightened. Scared out of her mind. As if her self-control was slipping away, bit by bit, with each sob emanating from the hall.

This was insane.

Her throat pinched, tight and dry. Her knees felt liquid. She clutched the wall, trying to keep herself on her feet. The DVD fell from her fingers.

"I'll take that." A man stepped from behind the jog in the wall that had concealed him from her view. He bent down and retrieved the DVD from the floor.

She forced her voice to work, forced her tongue to curl around the words. "No…evidence…police property…"

He straightened, the DVD in hand, as if

he hadn't heard her. Or just didn't care what she said.

"Stop." She pulled out her weapon. Confusion swirled with fear. She couldn't shoot him. He wasn't threatening her. Yet she couldn't let him take the disk. Not when they were so close to finding out the truth. She had to stop—

The barrel of her gun bobbed, her hands shaking. Her palms were so slick she could hardly keep hold of the gun. She couldn't control it. She couldn't control her own thoughts, her own body.

Oh God, she was going to die.

Warmth seeped into her pants and trickled down her legs. But she couldn't think of that now. Not the humiliation, not what was happening to her, none of it. She was going to die. And there wasn't anything she could do about it.

The man took the weapon from her shaking hand and raised it high above his head.

A scream ripped through the air and echoed in her ears. A scream from her own throat—a scream of pure terror cut short by the thudding blow from the butt of her own gun.

Chapter Two

Detective Randall McClellan of the Maryland State Police leaned forward in his chair, nailing his supervisor with his most sincere and forceful stare. "I went through the debriefing, Nick. I surrendered my weapon. I'm cooperating with the investigation. Isn't that enough? Do you have to put me on administrative leave, too?"

Detective Sergeant Nick Johnson raised a brow, his only answer.

Rand hated when he did that. "Come on, Nick. I don't need a vacation. Not while we're still finding out exactly what happened at Cranesbrook."

"You know what you have to do."

A sick feeling stirred deep in his stomach. "Talk to a shrink."

"They don't call them shrinks anymore."

"I don't care what they call them. I don't need one. I'm fine."

"I asked you to talk to someone after Richard was killed. Now that you shot his killer, I have to insist. You need a sense of closure."

The hollow feeling at the base of his throat widened at the thought of his dead partner. His former friend. "I got all the closure I needed when I shot Edmonston."

"You're not helping yourself here."

Rand blew out a long breath. It wouldn't be the first time his smart-ass mouth landed him in trouble. Not that he wasn't treading dangerously close to trouble already through no fault of his own. "I know the media is saying I shot Sid Edmonston to get revenge for Richard's death. But that's not the case and you know it. He would have killed Lily and Gage Darnell if I hadn't taken him out."

"I'm not worried about that. I'm worried about you. We have regulations for a reason, policies in place to help officers cope. I really should be putting you on administrative leave for a good long time."

"Then, why aren't you?"

"Because I need you." Nick gave him a pointed look and slid his ancient government-issue telephone across the desk. "Make an appointment."

Rand stared at the phone, a bitter taste rising in his throat. If there was anything he hated more than people with no regard for the law, it was sitting around talking about his feelings. Just the thought of wallowing in a mud pit of emotion while some junior Freud sat back and analyzed him gave him hives. He could just see the spark of excitement in the analyst's eyes when the subject of his father came up.

"Here's the number." Nick slid a paper bearing a list of therapists who worked with the department. "Either call or go home and start catching up on your sleep."

Rand glanced down at the names. He actually felt sick to his stomach. "If I do this, I'm back on the case?"

"If you do this, there's a woman you need to talk to waiting in the conference room."

"A woman? Who?"

"Brayden Sloane's sister."

So that was why Nick was willing to take shortcuts to get him back on the job. Brayden Sloane had been one of three men caught in an explosion at Cranesbrook. After that explosion, all hell had broken loose. The difference between Sloane and the other two men was that Sloane was missing.

"And all I have to do is set up an appointment?"

"Seems easy, doesn't it?"

Easy. Right.

"And there's one more thing."

"What?"

"We got a call from the St. Stephens PD. One of their officers discovered a DVD at Cranesbrook Associates. It appears to contain the missing surveillance video from the explosion in Lab 7."

"The missing video?" Rand shot to his feet. "Where was it found?"

"In Sid Edmonston's office. Hidden in the closet wall."

"Damn. This is big. This is huge. That video should show who caused the explosion. It might finally explain why Sid Edmonston was so desperate to cover it up." Desperate enough to kill.

Nick held up a hand. "Not so fast." He nodded to Rand's chair.

Rand sank into it. So there was more. And it wasn't good. "What haven't you told me?"

"We no longer have the DVD."

"Why? What happened to it?"

"Someone took it. No doubt the same someone who killed the officer who called it in."

"Killed?" Another officer murdered in conjunction with the same case? A weight bore down on Rand's chest. He might have shot the bastard who killed Richard, but this wasn't over. "Who was the officer?"

"A young patrol cop. Very promising, I guess. Her name was Maxine Wallace."

"Maxie!" Her curly red hair and twinkling eyes flashed through Rand's mind. It couldn't be Maxie. She was so full of life and energy and determination, he couldn't possibly imagine her dead. "You're sure?"

Nick nodded.

Rand swallowed, the aching hollowness in his throat growing. First Richard, now Maxie.

He thrust to his feet.

"Where the hell do you think you're going?"

"I have to get to Cranesbrook."

"Not until you have a word with Echo Sloane. And you're not doing that until…" He slid the phone closer to the desk's edge.

Damn. Rand grabbed the receiver and punched in the first number on Nick's list.

BALANCING her squirming baby daughter on her hip, Echo Sloane looked at her watch for what had to be the billionth time. The state trooper who had shown her to this small conference room had promised to fetch a detective to talk to her. But as the minutes ticked by, she wondered how sincere that promise had been.

She hated relying on other people for help. Bray had been missing for more than a week, and she hadn't found any sign of him. Nor had she found a sign that anyone else cared he was missing. Not the St. Stephens police, and now not the state. She felt so helpless, she could scream.

She looked down into her daughter's round face framed by wispy baby hair just getting long enough to curl. "We'll find your uncle Bray, Zoe. I promise. I'm just not sure how." However she managed, it was clear that relying on the police wasn't getting her anywhere. She was on her own. She walked to the door and grasped the knob.

It turned under her hand.

She stepped back and let the door open wide.

A tall, dark-haired man in a navy suit entered. Looking like a star from some gritty police drama, he narrowed flinty eyes and pressed his lips into an authoritative line. "Detective Rand McClellan. I'm sorry you had to wait so long."

He didn't look sorry. He looked emotionless. Just one more brick wall like the many she'd run into since Bray had disappeared. "The last state police detective I talked to said he would keep me informed about the search for my brother. I haven't heard a word since."

"There's nothing to tell. However, I do have some questions."

"You haven't found anything at all?"

"No."

"Have you been looking?" She knew she shouldn't be snippy with a man in a position to help, but she couldn't seem to bite the words back. She was getting so frustrated she could barely keep from screaming. "Because it seems to me you've been doing a lot of nothing."

One side of his lips twitched as if he was suppressing a smile. Or a comment he might regret. "Take my word for it, Ms. Sloane, we've been doing more than nothing. Now for those questions." He pulled a notebook from the inside pocket of his suitcoat and flipped it open. Another dip into the pocket and he held a pen.

"Another detective already asked me a bunch of questions."

"I have more."

She was sick of questions with no answers. Worry with no relief. But what was she going to do? If answering more questions had even the slightest chance of helping find Bray, she'd take a swing at anything he could throw. At least she would be doing *something,* getting *somewhere.* "Ask away. Although I don't know what I can tell you that I didn't already tell the other detective."

Zoe squealed and threw her body forward, trying to reach the floor and crawl. "Pay. Pay."

Apparently the ten-month-old was as tired of waiting as her mother. "Take it easy, sweetheart. You can play as soon as we're done here."

Detective McClellan nodded to the round table in the little room. "Would you like to sit down? Your baby seems like a handful."

"She's fine."

As if to prove her mother's words were

true, Zoe grabbed Echo's hair. Wrapping the mix of brown and blond strands around her fingers, she stuck her thumb in her mouth.

Echo smiled down at her little angel baby. When she looked back up, the detective's eyes were focused on her, his gaze so intense she suddenly felt exposed.

He cleared his throat but didn't look away. "When you talked to Detective Francis, the only friend of your brother's that you named was Gage Darnell."

Of course, his questions. "Bray had friends in the service, but since he got out, the only one he kept in contact with was Gage."

"What about women?"

"He didn't date much. He always said he was too busy with the business." And he was, but that wasn't the whole story. She'd known the truth. That after Zoe's father walked out, leaving Echo alone and pregnant, Bray had spent what little free time Five Star Security left him helping her get back on her feet. Guilt tightened the base of her throat.

"How long has he been out of the service?"

"Three years. That's when he started Five Star."

"Three years is a long time to be celibate."

"Maybe for a man." She'd just as soon stay celibate the rest of her life.

He curved a dark brow. "I was under the impression your brother is a man."

Her cheeks heated. She didn't know what it was about Detective McClellan that made her feel so threatened. Maybe it was the prospect of relying on someone to help her. Or the way he looked at her. Or the simple fact that he was one of the most attractive men she'd ever seen. Whatever it was, she had to get her act together. She needed to find Bray, and the detective could help. But if she didn't curb her inner bitchiness, she was going to alienate him. "I think something happened while he was overseas. Anyway, since he's been back, he's steered clear of relationships."

"How about people who worked at Cranesbrook?"

She searched her memory. "There was one. But she isn't a girlfriend. He didn't like her much."

"Did he give you a name?"

"Claire Fan...something. Fanshaw. I think she works in the computer division."

He scribbled a note. "What did he say about her?"

"It's not what you think. They weren't having some torrid affair. The only time Bray mentioned her name was to tell me how she was demanding to have security clearance into computer files that even *he* wasn't cleared to view."

"But he did mention her. By name."

"To tell me she was acting like a demanding brat."

He scrawled more notes before directing that penetrating gaze back to her.

She wanted to squirm in her chair. The man seemed to have little emotion of his own. Instead, he had the disturbing ability to home in on every word, every shiver of emotion she felt. He made her feel totally exposed. As if she was naked in front of him, though he was buttoned up in a three-piece suit.

"Have you noticed your brother acting strange recently?"

"Strange? How?"

"Tense. Nervous. Anything out of the ordinary."

She fought the urge to pace. The truth was, Bray was always tense. Especially since he'd gotten out of the service. But that wasn't surprising. Starting a security company was stressful, not to mention the stress she'd inadvertently piled on him. If Bray was nervous and tense, it was because of her. "He seemed the same as always."

The detective held her gaze, as if he didn't quite buy it and was waiting for her to come clean.

The sound of her heartbeat pulsed in her ears, ticking off the seconds. Could he read what she was really thinking? Did he know the guilt she felt?

Finally he dropped his gaze to his notebook. "Was your brother experiencing any personal problems that you know about?"

These questions just got better and better. "No."

"You're sure?"

She wasn't. Not really. Knowing Bray, even if he was experiencing some personal problems, he probably wouldn't tell her. He wouldn't want to add to her burden. "He didn't say anything to me about personal problems."

"How about financial problems?"

At least she could answer that one. "He didn't have financial problems. He saved a lot of money while he was in the service. And Five Star was very successful."

The detective scribbled more notes, then turned that stare back on her. That stare that saw so much, yet gave away so little. "Did your brother talk to you about any frustrations he was experiencing with his contract for security at Cranesbrook Associates?"

She might not be able to read the detective's emotionless features, but she could read his questions. "Why are you asking about all this stuff?"

"Standard questions."

"Standard for a suspect, maybe."

He didn't react.

"That's it, isn't it?" Her stomach seized. The headlines in this morning's newspaper flashed through her mind. McClellan was the detective in the paper. The detective who'd shot the Cranesbrook president. The detective who'd uncovered the explosion in one of the Cranesbrook labs. "Bray was caught in that explosion. You can't think he *caused* it."

"I think whatever the evidence leads me to think."

"Evidence?" Her voice cracked with anger. He couldn't have any evidence. Bray did nothing wrong.

Zoe stared up at her with wide eyes.

"Then why hasn't he turned up? In a hospital? In a morgue? He hasn't even tried to contact you. Those things alone are enough to arouse suspicion."

She shook her head. She couldn't

believe he was suggesting this. "My brother is a good man."

"Good men can get caught up in unsavory things, Ms. Sloane." If she wasn't mistaken, a flicker of sympathy warmed those dark eyes.

Sympathy she didn't want or need. "Bray would never do anything to hurt people."

"Your brother was a soldier. Special Forces. I suspect he's capable of many things, some that involve hurting people."

"But he wouldn't. He's a good man. The only good man I've ever known."

"I'm sorry."

He looked as if he meant it this time, but that didn't make Echo feel one bit better. "You're wrong about Bray. I'll prove it." And she would. If only she had the first inkling how.

Zoe looked up at her through squinted eyes. Her face crumpled, and a stuttered cry broke from her lips.

Echo struggled to keep from breaking into tears herself. "It's okay, sweetheart.

Everything's okay." But Zoe continued to cry, as if she recognized Echo's reassurances for the empty lies they were.

Chapter Three

Rand shouldn't have been thinking about Echo Sloane as he entered the administration wing of Cranesbrook Associates' main building. God knew he had plenty to occupy his mind. But somehow he couldn't wipe away the look of helpless frustration on her heart-shaped face when she'd figured out her brother was a suspect.

She obviously adored Sloane. And that was what had dug into Rand's chest. Because if Bray Sloane had a role in whatever Sid Edmonston had been trying to keep quiet at Cranesbrook, Rand didn't want to think how devastating that would be for Echo.

He shook his head, trying to dislodge

the thought. He shouldn't care. He couldn't. Whether Echo Sloane was hurt wasn't his business. His business was finding out who killed Maxie Wallace. His business was stopping whoever had taken up Sid Edmonston's murderous mantle. His business was getting to the bottom of this Cranesbrook mess and ending it once and for all.

The possibility of Echo Sloane getting hurt in the process couldn't be his concern.

A state trooper Rand didn't know stood in the hall outside Edmonston's office. Rand gave his name, and the trooper jotted it in the log book, along with the time he arrived.

"Who was stationed here when Officer Wallace was killed?" he asked the trooper.

"Cop from St. Stephens. Detective Farrell already talked to him. At least, he tried."

"Tried?"

"The kid was crying. Couldn't stop. Was like that when we found him, before anybody knew Wallace was dead."

Strange. And definitely something to follow up. "Thanks." Rand moved past the trooper and continued to the office where he'd shot a man only yesterday.

Entering through the shattered glass door, he stepped over the bloodstain on the carpet without so much as a twinge for the bastard who left it. He only wished the murder spree had ended with the crooked president's death. He only wished another cop hadn't died. He stepped into the inner office of the suite.

The first thing he saw was Maxie's curly red hair. The next was the blood. She lay on her side, curled into the fetal position, her eyes wide with fear and clouded with death.

Pressure bore down on his chest. No matter how he prided himself on controlling his emotions, he couldn't pass over this death without feeling the ache of grief all the way to his bones. Maxie Wallace was a fellow cop and a good one. And the thought that some bastard had stolen her life was an unspeakable tragedy. That it had happened on the heels of Richard's death was nearly too much to bear.

The medical examiner glanced up at

him. A woman in her midfifties, she sized Rand up with eyes that had seen the result of far too much violence. "McClellan, right? Want to take a look? I'm just about to remove the body."

The body. Not "Maxie," not even "her." The woman who a short time ago had been bursting with life was no more than "the body" now. "Cause of death?"

"You're going to have to wait for my autopsy report to get the official word. But from the look of it, I'd say blunt-force trauma to the head."

"She was beaten to death with her own gun." Detective Dean Farrell stepped out of the small closet tucked behind the wide mahogany desk. "Just the way that janitor was killed. But I guess we can't attribute this to Sid Edmonston."

"No, guess not." Rand didn't relish the idea of working with Dean Farrell on this case. He was a good enough detective, but as good as the guy might be, he was no Richard Francis. He and Francis had been so used to each other, they'd often read each other's minds. "You finished with the photos?"

"Yeah."

"Were the tech guys here?"

"Just left."

"No chance you found that DVD she reported."

"Nope. My guess? The person who killed her has it."

Rand nodded. His conclusion also. The question was, how did the murderer get in? And what did that video reveal that was worth killing for? "Was anyone else in this building?"

"Most employees got the day off. I guess that's one of the perks when the company president dies." He shrugged a shoulder. "Seems like a lot to go through to get a vacation."

In normal circumstances, Rand might joke right along with Farrell. But with Richard Francis already dead and Maxie lying only a few feet away, he didn't have the stomach for it. "I'll check out whoever made it in."

"You know her?" He nodded in the direction of Maxie's body.

"Yeah."

"Then get. I'll finish up here."

Rand let his thanks hang in the air unsaid and turned away. He'd thought he could handle seeing Maxie. He'd been wrong. But it wasn't grief that got to him. Or even the recent sting of losing Richard Francis. Whenever he looked at her battered face, all he could think about was the extra role he'd given her in the original murder at the mental hospital, the murder that had led him to Cranesbrook. And he couldn't help feel that if he hadn't called on her help, she'd still be alive.

Taking one last glance, he left the office and made his way down the deserted hall. As he drew closer to the computer department offices, the click of a keyboard broke the silence. He walked past the vacant support staff office and followed the sound through an open door.

Inside the small office labeled Supervisor of Computer Operations, he found a lone woman staring at a computer screen. Her wavy, shoulder-length hair matched the red cherry finish of her desk and credenza. He eyed the name plate on her desk. Bingo. "Claire Fanshaw?"

She pivoted in her chair and narrowed green eyes on him. "McClellan, right? Your picture was in the paper this morning."

"Don't believe everything you read."

"Never do."

"I need to ask you a few questions."

She brushed her hair back from her face. "What's going on? I saw an ambulance and a crime-tech truck come through the gate."

"What else did you see?"

"Nothing. I've been in here all day. I just noticed the commotion through the window. So what happened?"

He ignored her question. "*Who* did you see this morning?"

"Just Dr. Kelso." She checked her watch, a sparkly number. Probably expensive. "He left pretty early. Several hours ago. I'm not sure of the time."

So the director of the computer division

had been here. Rand made a note. "Any-one else?"

"Anyone who dared come to work was probably snared in police tape on the way in."

"Except you."

"I brought a pair of scissors." Her lips flickered in a guarded smile. "I had a lot of important work to do."

"Have you ever heard the name Project Cypress?" Gage Darnell had told him the name of the project being developed in the lab where the explosion took place. But neither Darnell nor Rand knew what it was. Hopefully Claire would.

"Project Cypress?" She looked directly at him, as if she didn't have anything to hide.

Right. He'd dealt with enough criminals to know a false innocent act when he smelled one. Even if it was delivered by an obviously practiced liar. "I can tell you recognize the name, so you might as well drop the act."

"Sorry." She had the good grace to look a little sheepish. "I don't work in the lab. I don't know much about the individual projects. Even if I did, I couldn't tell you. Cranesbrook works on top secret projects. I could lose my job. Or worse."

"Worse?"

She shifted in her chair, the overhead light reflecting off a glittery scarf draped around the neck of her plain sweater. "It's the latest thing. The government likes to go after people who leak information. Haven't you noticed?"

He was pretty sure she'd had something more specific in mind than the current political atmosphere. Of course, getting it out of her was another thing altogether. She obviously didn't trust easily. "Are you saying Project Cypress is part of a government contract?"

"Most of what Cranesbrook does is part of a government contract. And I only have the clearance to know about a fraction of it."

And judging from her habit of answering questions with questions, she'd like to know more. "What if I told you what I know? Would you be willing to share then?"

She perked up, suddenly all ears. "Maybe."

"Project Cypress was being developed in Lab 7, the lab where the recent accident took place. As a result of the accident, two men were hurt and one disappeared, and the president of Cranesbrook killed three men to cover up the accident."

"Three? I heard he killed a janitor and a detective. Who's the third?"

"A security guard. He died in a hit-and-run. We didn't know it was related until we searched Edmonston's house last night and found blood and dents on the front fender of his car. Same blood type. As soon as we have a DNA match, we'll release the information to the public."

He watched Claire, trying to gauge if he was reaching her. Hard to say. "Another thing the public doesn't know quite yet is that there has been another murder. This morning. Right in this building."

Claire sucked in a breath. "Who?"

"A police officer who was gathering evidence."

She pressed her lips together, a small crease digging between her brows. "So it wasn't just Edmonston."

"No."

"Do you have a suspect?"

"That I can't share with you at this time. But I do know some other things. For instance, I know you've been trying to get a higher security clearance recently. And I'm guessing it was so you could take a peek at Project Cypress." He might be making a leap, basing his pronouncement on a hunch he'd gotten while talking to Echo Sloane, but he sensed if he wanted answers from a woman as guarded as Claire Fanshaw, he'd have to swing for the fence.

She shook her head. "Your guess is wrong. I need the higher clearance to do my job."

"Brayden Sloane didn't see it that way."

Her lips tightened at the name. "It only makes sense for me to have the higher clearance. Bray might have been able to influence Dr. Kelso, but he wouldn't even listen to me."

Rand smiled. Now he might be getting somewhere. "Do you think Bray had a personal reason for refusing to help you get clearance?"

"A personal reason? I don't know."

"Is there anything about those files you might notice that others wouldn't? Like exactly when the files were accessed? And by whom?"

"You think Bray might have accessed the Project Cypress files and wanted to cover his tracks?"

He could see the wheels turning behind those green eyes. "Is it possible?"

"I don't know. I don't know him very well. You're thinking the accident might be some kind of corporate sabotage?"

He didn't know. All he had were guesses. "Was Project Cypress worth sabotaging?"

She chewed on her bottom lip and stared at the computer monitor.

"Whatever you tell me won't leave this room. You have my word," he said.

She didn't budge. Even when the computer's power-save feature made the screen go dark.

"We had a deal, Claire. I trusted you

with information I shouldn't have shared. Now it's time you trust me." He held out his hands, palms up. "Don't protect people like Sid Edmonston."

She released her lip and let out a sigh. Looking past Rand, she peered out the office door as if to check that the coast was clear. "I don't know what Project Cypress is. But I did see something about it."

"What?"

"You've heard of performance bonuses?"

Rand nodded.

"The deal for Project Cypress works kind of like that. If the project is completed by a certain deadline, the researchers involved get a significant bonus."

"How much?"

"Ten million dollars."

Not chump change, that was for sure. "What is the date?"

"That's the interesting part. About two months ago the date was moved up and the bonus was doubled. The project will bring in an extra twenty mil if it's completed by next week."

Next week. That was enough time pressure to cause an accident. An accident that needed to be covered up. Even if that meant some people had to die. "And if it isn't completed by the date? What happens then?"

"They forfeit the money."

He thought about Bray Sloane. If the explosion was caused by researchers rushing to meet the deadline, it would mean Sloane was simply a victim of the accident like Gage Darnell. It wouldn't explain his disappearance, but at least Rand wouldn't be responsible for breaking Echo's heart. "Who stands to profit from this kind of arrangement?"

"The way it's set up, most of the bonus goes to the researchers working on the project. And management, of course."

"Like Sid Edmonston."

She nodded. "Now I suppose his share will be split between Dr. Kelso and the director of research, Dr. Ulrich."

"And you said the researchers? Would that include Hank Riddell?" Rand had suspected from the first that Riddell was in this neck deep.

"Of course. There was another researcher, too. But he left the company recently."

"Do you have his name?"

"Ellroy. Mac Ellroy."

Rand wrote it down. "How about Wes Vanderhoven? Do lab technicians share in the bonus?"

"Sure. Of course, Hank and Wes probably don't know the exact dollar amount. Management keeps that information pretty close to the vest."

"How do *you* know about it?"

"Um, I…stumbled upon it."

"Stumbled, huh?"

"Another murder, huh?" she countered. "I'll bet I can guess who's on your suspect list."

"Don't worry. I won't tell anyone about your clumsiness." He pulled out his card, not even bothering to suppress a chuckle. "If you happen to stumble again, give me a call."

She took the card.

On the way out of the office, he plucked one of hers from a card holder on her secretary's desk. He couldn't wait to hear what Wesley Vanderhoven had to say about the time pressure he'd been under to complete Project Cypress.

Rand smiled and shook his head. Who could have guessed he would be so eager to march into the loony bin?

BRACING HIMSELF, Rand pushed through the gleaming glass doors of the Beech Grove Clinic mental hospital. His eagerness to step into this place had cooled a bit on the drive from Cranesbrook. He still wanted to talk to Vanderhoven. But after spending so much time here investigating the murder of the janitor, he was beginning to feel like Nurse Dumont was sizing him up for his own custom straitjacket.

He caught up with the nurse halfway down the main hall. "How's Wes Vanderhoven today? I trust he's not still under sedation?"

Nurse Dumont peered over her glasses,

her short brown hair sticking tight to her head as if glued. Her lips puckered with distaste. "Your storm troopers were here. Though what you think our financial records are going to tell you about Sid Edmonston is beyond me."

Ah, the search warrant finally came through. They'd combed the premises after the janitor's death, discovering the janitorial closet where he'd been killed, but getting access to the clinic's records had taken longer. "Along with Gage Darnell's medical records, we should be able to learn something. Have you gotten the signed release form from Darnell?"

Her glower told him she had. "He picked the records up himself."

"Darnell did?"

"If you want them, ask him."

He would, after a chat with Vanderhoven. He started walking down the hall.

"He's been moved."

Rand turned around and met Nurse Dumont's hard stare with one of his own. "Then I'll follow you."

She didn't move.

"Unless you would rather I bring in some help and take a look through the whole place again?"

"There's nothing left for you to search." A deep voice emerged from the office, followed by Dr. Morton. Next to the strapping Nurse Dumont, Morton looked small, however he was anything but meek. "Truly, Detective, I don't know what you hope to accomplish by harassing us. We have nothing to hide."

Rand eyed the man that Gage Darnell had accused of keeping him prisoner in the clinic. Morton was dirty. Rand could feel it. He just hadn't been able to prove it. Yet. "Then you won't mind showing me to Wesley Vanderhoven's new room."

"He might be a little foggy. The medication he's on has that effect."

The strong scent of peppermint reached Rand, carried on Morton's breath. Rand's stomach gave a buck. "He's not still sedated, is he?"

"Of course not. He's recovering from

his ordeal nicely. But that doesn't mean he has returned to normal."

Rand doubted anyone could return to normal inside these walls; although, he would be willing to bet that under Morton's care, Vanderhoven had a bigger challenge than most. He only had to think of the things Gage Darnell had told him about his forced stay at Beech Grove to know that. He had to find a way to get Vanderhoven out.

But first he needed to have a talk with him. "Take me to his room."

Morton nodded to the nurse, the fluorescent light glinting off scalp visible through his thinning blond hair. "Nurse Dumont will be happy to."

One side of her pale lips lifted in a snarl. Launching into a march, she brushed past him and headed down the hall. Two turns later she stopped at a door and knocked. "Mr. Vanderhoven?" she said in a sugary voice Rand never could have imagined coming from her lips. "You have a visitor."

She pushed the door open a few inches.

Without sparing Rand a glance, she hurried back down the hall, the rapid squeak of her shoes fading.

Rand pushed the door wide and stepped into the room.

The familiar theme song from *Star Trek: The Next Generation* soared from the television suspended from the ceiling. From the hospital bed, pale eyes watched him from an even paler face. "I know you, don't I?" the man asked.

He doubted it. The times Rand had tried to talk to Vanderhoven, the lab tech had been so out of it, he hadn't seemed able to recognize himself. "I'm Detective Rand McClellan with the Maryland State Police. I need to ask you some questions about the accident you were involved in at Cranesbrook."

Vanderhoven let his head fall back into the pillow with a heavy sigh.

"My partner and I were here before. I'm glad to see you're doing better." Of course, *better* was a relative word. Although only twenty-six, the lab technician looked about fifteen years older. His cheeks were gaunt under sharp cheekbones, and circles dark as bruises cupped his eyes.

"Thanks. They said I was in bad shape when they brought me in."

"They?"

"Dr. Morton and the nurses."

Gage's story of being restrained and drugged flashed in the back of Rand's mind. "Has the staff here kept you confined in any way?"

"Confined? Like how?"

"Have they restrained you? Prevented you from leaving or reaching friends or family?"

"No. I mean, they've sedated me. I know that. But I was very upset and confused when I woke up. I guess they didn't have a choice."

Upset and confused. That was basically how Gage had described how he'd felt upon awaking. "So you've never had your hands and legs restrained?"

"Not that I remember."

Rand nodded. The condition Vanderhoven had been in, maybe they hadn't had to worry about him escaping. "Have you been in contact with anyone from outside the clinic?"

"I've talked to people at work. Hank Riddell came to see me."

Rand made a note. The fact that Hank Riddell had been observing at the hospital the night the janitor had been killed had bothered Rand from the beginning. Sid Edmonston had confessed to killing the janitor, but the possibility that Hank Riddell had assisted him seemed more than probable.

And maybe he was the one who killed Maxie.

"Any friends come to see you? Family?"

"Most of my friends are guys I game with online. As far as friends I see in person, Hank is it." He shrugged a bony shoulder. "Work is my family."

Cranesbrook sure hadn't felt very familylike to him. Or even particularly friendly. He hated to see a guy so all alone in the world stuck here in the hospital under Morton's thumb. "Have you been watching the news lately?"

"You mean have I seen the stories about

the murder that happened here? And the manhunt for the Cranesbrook security guy, Darnell?"

Apparently he had. "If you're uncomfortable with what has been happening around here or your medical care, I can arrange for you to be transferred to another facility. All you have to do is say the word." At least until Rand could manage to get a court order. Then he could have Vanderhoven moved regardless.

"Not necessary. I'm fine here. Cranesbrook's insurance company is paying for the whole thing. Besides, I'm feeling stronger already."

"Then you'll be strong enough to answer my questions. I'd like you to start by telling me everything you remember happening leading up to the accident."

"Leading up to it? I was in the lab, working. Same as every day."

"What were you working on?"

"It's classified."

"Listen, I'm going to be straight with you here, Wes. The president of Cranesbrook tried very hard to cover up the accident you were involved in. He wanted to cover it up so badly, he killed people. I have to know what you were working on."

Vanderhoven's prominent Adam's apple bobbed in his skinny throat. "Can't tell you. I'll get in big trouble."

Frustration knotted Rand's gut. Except for his enlightening conversation with Claire Fanshaw, trying to break through the wall of silence surrounding Cranesbrook was like chipping at a brick wall with a toothpick. "Were you under recent pressure to meet deadlines in your research?"

"There are always deadlines."

"Was there recent pressure? More pressure than usual?"

"What are you getting at?"

"I have reason to believe time pressure might have caused you or your colleagues to take shortcuts. Shortcuts that could lead to an accident."

"I didn't take shortcuts. Dr. Ulrich, the director of research, is the best in the country—no, the best in the world. He never would have pressed any of us to take shortcuts." Vanderhoven's face flushed pink. He gripped the sheets in his fists, then released them, gripped and released. "I didn't bring this on myself."

He hated upsetting someone in Vanderhoven's condition, but he couldn't back down now. He needed some answers. "I'll leave you alone in a moment. First I want you to tell me what you remember about the explosion."

"Nothing. I was knocked out. I woke up here." He stared at Rand as if his patience was spent. "Like I said, I'm tired."

Rand's face heated. Annoyance surged through him, working from his gut into his tightened fists. If Vanderhoven didn't start coming up with some answers, Rand was going to have to put his hands around that turkey neck and squeeze the answers out of him. He took a step toward the bed.

What the hell was he doing?

He shook his head and forced a breath into tight lungs. He didn't get rattled. He didn't get carried away with frustration or any other emotion. Yet for a second there, he'd actually contemplated choking a witness merely because the poor guy couldn't remember what had happened while he was unconscious.

Of course, aggression could be a by-product of severe stress.

He shook the thought away. The shrink he had to meet with tomorrow would love that thought. Too bad he wouldn't be sharing it.

He focused on Vanderhoven. "Just a few more questions, and I'll let you rest. Can you try to remember what you saw when you woke up? Anything? Even if it seemed like a dream?"

"Dreams? Yeah, I had some dreams. I don't know if I can explain them very well, but I'll do my best." Again he stared at Rand, those light-blue eyes burning and chilling at the same time. "I had the kind of dreams you have in a place like this. A mental hospital. You know, the kind where I was screaming and screaming, and yet no one could hear me. No one would come."

Emotion swept over Rand like an icy draft. Not the flame of anger this time, but the chill of fear. He sucked in a deep breath and tried to push it back, the way he had the anger.

What was happening to him?

Vanderhoven kept staring, kept talking in that tortured voice. "And then there were hands holding me down. Hands I couldn't see. But as much as I struggled, I couldn't get away."

Rand could feel the hands, pinning him down. It was so real. Panic surged through him, hot and mindless. He had to get out of here. He had to get away. Yet what was he getting away from?

This was crazy. He wasn't an emotional man. He was cold. Logical. He didn't know what the hell was happening to him, but he had to get it under control.

"And I couldn't breathe. No matter how hard I tried, I couldn't get enough oxygen. Have you ever had that feeling?"

Rand's chest tightened and along with it came the grip of fear. Every reaction he had to Vanderhoven's story seemed to balloon out of control. Every emotion that flickered, however small, seemed to engulf him and sweep him away.

He gripped the notebook until the spiral wire binding bit into his hands, giving him something to focus on, something to cut through the emotion.

"Then harsh voices started whispering in my ears," Vanderhoven continued. "It was horrible. They told me I was a worthless failure. That I should have died in the explosion. That I should just kill myself now."

Again a wave of feeling swept over Rand. And this time it was accompanied by memories of his own. His father had talked about voices like that. He said those voices came to him in dreams. Dreams of worthlessness. Dreams of failure. Dreams fueled by his depression.

Grief clogged Rand's throat. Guilt. He tried to push it away, but this time he couldn't do it. He gripped the notebook, but the pain did no good. All he could think about was his dad in the weeks before his death. The way his face hollowed out under sharp cheekbones and sunken eyes. The sound of a grown man sobbing. The smell of gunpowder and blood and splattered brains on the night he'd swallowed his shotgun.

A sob worked up Rand's throat. Guilt clamped around his neck like cold hands.

"Have you ever felt like you wanted to kill yourself, Detective?"

Kill himself. Maybe that's what he should do. Just end it, like his dad had. Maybe that was the only way out of this raging emotional hell.

Maybe that was the only way.

Chapter Four

Rand lifted his head from the steering wheel of his vehicle and stared through the dirty windshield at the clinic. Thank God, he'd gotten out of there. His back was wet with sweat and his blood was still jittering in his veins, but at least the thoughts had subsided. He was slowly crawling out of the pit of depression.

What the hell had happened?

It didn't make sense. None of it. He wasn't an emotional man. An old girlfriend had once called him cold. Not a good thing in her book, but it had served him pretty well. He sure as hell was nothing like his old man. Nothing.

Then why had he contemplated killing himself?

Hell, he hadn't just contemplated it. He'd decided to do it. *He'd decided to commit suicide.*

Was it nothing more than stress? God, he wished he could believe that. But even though he'd heard about the strange effects on the psyche that stress and lack of sleep could have, deciding to commit suicide seemed a bit beyond the typical nervous breakdown.

Or was it? Was this what a nervous breakdown was?

Could he finally be losing it? Could Richard's death and shooting Sid Edmonston have taken more of a toll on him than even Nick had feared? Could seeing Maxie Wallace's body have been the final push that sent him over the edge? Was he going down the same dark path as his father?

A dark path he'd helped push his father off?

He shook his head. There had to be some

other explanation. Something happening within those walls.

Something happening within those walls...

He started the car. Gage Darnell had agreed to help with the investigation. And it was about time Rand took him up on it.

THE SCENT of freshly brewed coffee swept over Rand as he entered the lobby of Five Star Security. He'd downed two cups on the drive to Baltimore, but after what he'd been through, he needed more. And he needed it strong.

"Hello, Detective." The friendliness in Peggy Olson's voice nearly knocked him over. Apparently since Rand had cleared Darnell of murder charges, he'd gone from villain to hero in the office manager's eyes. "Want some coffee?"

"Love some." He looked through the sliding window and into the main office. Except for the two employees sitting at desks surrounded by security monitors tapped into businesses all around Baltimore, Peggy seemed to be the only one here. "Is Gage around?"

"He's in his office catching up." She handed him a steaming foam cup and started back toward the private offices. "I'll tell him you're here."

"Thanks."

Rand had just taken his first sip when Gage appeared. "Detective. What's going on? Any news about Bray?"

"No. I need to ask you a few more questions about Cranesbrook and the Beech Grove Clinic."

"Come on back. I was just typing some notes into my computer about everything that's happened. It helps me think. I'm also working on hacking into Cranesbrook's files."

Rand held up a hand. "I don't want to hear about that. Not officially, anyway."

Gage gave a knowing nod and led Rand to a room filled with a nice-size desk and comfortable chairs. They each took a chair. As soon as they sat, Gage leaned forward, his dark brows pinching with concern. "So what do you need?"

"More about what you experienced at Beech Grove."

"This might help." He opened a desk drawer and pulled out an envelope. He shoved it across the desk to Rand. "My medical records from Beech Grove."

Rand opened the envelope and leafed through the photocopies inside. Nothing resembling what he'd experienced jumped out at him. "How about what you remember?"

A dark cloud seemed to pass over Darnell. "I already told you all of it. I was tied down. Sedated much of the time."

"Did you experience any emotional problems?"

"Emotional problems? Like what?"

"Fear. Depression. Nightmares that seemed real. Voices in your head. Maybe thoughts of suicide."

Darnell leaned back in his chair and stroked his jaw. "The whole thing was like a nightmare. Being tied down for days with no way to reach anyone, no way to even let

Lily know I was alive. That's pretty damn depressing. But you lost me on the voices and suicide. Did someone commit suicide? Vanderhoven?"

Rand shook his head. "I just talked to Vanderhoven. He's fine...well, considering the circumstances."

"Then what is all this depression and suicide stuff?"

"Things Vanderhoven described feeling in the days after the accident." Rand shifted. Of course, it wasn't just Vanderhoven.

"I didn't have any of those problems." Darnell's face tensed, as if even thinking about what he'd experienced still brought him pain. "I remember being very confused. Angry. Scared. I might add paranoid, but since people actually *were* out to kill me, that was more of a reality."

"You said there was an explosion. And that you experienced nausea and lost consciousness. But do you know if the other strange effects you felt were from the lab, or could you have been given something in the hospital? Something that caused your disorientation and emotional turmoil?"

"I don't know. I overheard some things when I was there. Enough to tell me Dr. Morton and Nurse Dumont were helping cover up the accident. Things like they were being paid to keep their mouths shut and keep Vanderhoven and me out of sight."

"But nothing about additional experimentation?"

"No. What makes you think it's a possibility?"

Because when I was talking to Vanderhoven today, I felt some strange things. Rand let the words run through his mind, but cut them off before they reached his lips. "Things Vanderhoven told me. But then, maybe he was more injured in the blast than you were."

"Maybe." A muscle twitched along Darnell's jaw. "I can't help worrying about what that means for Bray. He was caught in the blast, too. And with no medical attention afterward…"

Rand nodded. He'd considered the

possible outcomes for Sloane. And after meeting Echo, they'd burrowed into him like a sharp pain. If Sloane had a role in the explosion, he might deserve what he got, but Echo didn't deserve it. And Rand got the feeling that she'd been stuck with a lot of bad outcomes she didn't deserve. "What about Sloane? Was he tense before the accident?"

Darnell thought about the question, a pained look on his face. Finally he gave a reluctant nod. "He was a little tense. Maybe more short-tempered than usual. I thought it was just money pressure, like I told you before."

Money pressure. And yet Echo had sworn Bray was in good financial shape. "Do you have any reason to believe he was in debt?"

"He mentioned he was helping his sister. That's all. She had some pretty big medical bills."

Maybe that was why Echo didn't want to think her brother needed money. He needed the money to help her. Or maybe she didn't know about it. "Big medical bills, huh? What would the destruction of

Project Cypress be worth to a competing corporation?"

Darnell shook his head. "I don't know what Project Cypress is, but I do know Bray. And I just don't…"

"Even if he needed money for his sister?"

Darnell pinched the bridge of his nose between thumb and forefinger. "God, I don't think so. At least, I hope not. Have you asked Echo?"

"She doesn't want to face the possibility that her brother might have jaywalked at some point in his life."

Gage nodded. "Bray and Echo's father took off when Echo was pretty young. They're close."

And now she felt like Rand was trying to drag down her big brother. Rand forced his mind off Echo. He couldn't protect her feelings. God knew, he had a horrible track record on that score. "Did you see Sloane during the explosion?"

"He took Dr. Kelso out of the building and I entered the lab. That's the last I saw of him. Did you ask Vanderhoven?"

The memory of his emotional breakdown lurked in the back of his mind like a persistent headache. "I…didn't get the chance."

"Vanderhoven was in the lab before the explosion happened. By the time I got there, he was unconscious. And when I woke up after the explosion, he and Bray were gone. I don't know if he regained consciousness or Bray got him out or what happened exactly, but he might be able to tell you more than I can."

Great. Another trip to the nuthouse. Rand pushed himself up from his chair and walked to the door. "Let me know if you find anything in those Cranesbrook files. Off the record, of course."

"If I can get in this time, you mean."

"I get the idea you can do anything you set your mind to. You just need time to concentrate."

"You mean time without the law breathing down my neck?"

Rand gave him a grin. "Yeah. I'll focus on breathing down someone else's neck, someone who deserves it." And he couldn't help but hope that someone wasn't Bray Sloane—for Echo's sake.

Darnell rose from his chair. First to the door, he pulled it open for Rand and paused, his hand resting on the knob. "I know I agreed to stick around Baltimore in case you need me, Detective McClellan, but…"

Rand focused his attention on Darnell. "You planning to take a trip?"

"Just over the state line in Delaware. Rehoboth Beach. A place called the Sunrise Bed and Breakfast."

"Sounds nice."

Darnell shrugged a shoulder. "I'll take my laptop. I promised Lily we'd spend some uninterrupted time together. And I need to know she's safe."

"Not a bad idea. With some of the strange things going on around here…"

Darnell's brows arched toward his dark hair. "More strange things?"

Rand shook his head. He shouldn't have let that slip. He sure as hell didn't want to get into it. "You don't want to know."

Darnell opened his mouth, but the chirp

of a cell phone stalled his response. Releasing the door-knob, he pulled out his phone and checked the readout. A smile spread over his lips and glowed in his eyes. His wife's call, no doubt. "You're right, Detective. I don't want to know. I have all I can focus on right here."

Rand nodded and slipped out the door. Darnell had been through hell—a hell Rand had made worse by believing he was a murderer. The least Rand could do now was leave Darnell alone with his phone call.

Besides, Rand knew what he had to do next.

THE LAST PERSON Rand expected to see standing in the reception area of Beech Grove was Echo Sloane. But there she was, looking soft and feminine in a gauzy blouse and jeans. And ready to take on the world, judging from the determined set of her jaw.

"Echo." His body tensed as she turned to look at him. "Why are you here?"

"Hello to you, too, Detective." She lifted a hand to her face, shoving chestnut hair streaked with blond back from her eyes. "I could ask you the same question. And I'll bet we'd have the same answer."

"You're here to talk to Wesley Vanderhoven?"

"If he knows anything about what happened to Bray during the explosion, I need to find out. I need to help my brother." Her voice hitched on the last word.

She might be putting on a brave face, but underneath she was afraid of what she'd find. She should be. She could believe all she wanted that her brother was innocent, but each day that passed with no sign of him suggested otherwise. Unless, of course, he hadn't shown up because he was dead. "Listen, you don't have to look into this yourself."

"And what? I should leave it up to you?"

"It's my job."

"Funny, yesterday it seemed like your job was proving Bray did something wrong."

"I don't want to get into this with you, Echo. The evidence is the evidence. Whatever it shows is what I'll believe."

"As long as you don't twist it, that's fine with me." She crossed her arms.

Obviously she would never look at this rationally. "Where's Zoe?"

"She's at home with a babysitter. So you see, there's no reason I can't be here. And no way for you to keep me from talking to Mr. Vanderhoven. So if you think I'm just going to smile and let you shoo me away, you're crazy."

Crazy. Yesterday's breakdown flashed through his mind—and the prospect of having Echo as a witness if it happened again. Even more reason to convince her to leave Beech Grove. "I would never say you can't talk to Vanderhoven. But you have to realize this isn't a game. Several people have died as a result of their involvement in this case."

She raised her chin. "And I have to make sure Bray isn't one of them."

"I'm not talking about the danger to Bray. I'm talking about the danger to you. Sid Edmonston killed to keep the truth from coming out. But it didn't stop with him. There's been at least one death since. Asking questions is risky. Dangerous. Have you thought about that? Have you thought about what your daughter's life would be like without her mother?"

"That's a low blow."

"Maybe. But it's reality." And even as worried as Rand was about breaking down in front of Echo, the prospect of her becoming a victim of whatever was going on—like Richard, like Maxie—was worse.

She shifted her feet, the rubber soles of her athletic shoes squeaking on the waxed floor. Finally her chin came up once again, and she looked at him with determined gray eyes. "I have to find the truth. Bray would do it for me."

"That doesn't mean he'd want you to endanger yourself for him."

Her gaze wavered, then dropped to the floor.

"If I learn anything, I'll let you know."

She shook her head. "Don't bother. I'll talk to Mr. Vanderhoven after you're done."

"You haven't heard a word I said."

"I heard. And if I feel there's a danger, I'll be careful. But I love Bray. I believe in him. And I'm not going to turn my back on him. Not when he's never turned his back on me."

He blew a stream of air through tight lips and focused on the young nurse with short blond hair who was heading their way. He might not be able to talk Echo out of getting involved, but he could keep her from facing Vanderhoven and whatever else she ran into alone. At least then he could make sure she was safe. He might not be able to protect her from getting her faith in her brother dashed, but he could protect her physically. "If you have to do this, you might as well come with me."

She looked at him from the corner of her eye, as if she didn't trust what he was offering. Finally she nodded. "Okay."

"But I'll ask the questions."

"As long as you ask what needs to be asked, I won't make a peep."

He should leave it at that. Let her face whatever it was that Vanderhoven had to say. But somehow, he couldn't. Not without giving her a warning. "You know, if he does have information about your brother, it might be something you don't want to hear."

She raised her chin. "I'm used to facing things I don't want to, detective."

Fair enough. He certainly couldn't protect her from the truth. As much as he might feel he should. And if she had been able to keep herself from falling apart for the last week, she could probably handle ten more minutes.

He'd just better make sure *he* could do the same.

The young nurse reached them, and with her came a wave of lemon scent. Probably some sort of citrus shampoo. She gave him a confused look, the hair framing her face damp with sweat, as if she'd just finished a workout. "Ahh, Detective? Can I help you?"

He held up a hand. "We're here to talk to Wesley Vanderhoven. If Dr. Morton or Nurse Dumont has a problem with that, they'll know where to find me."

The nurse nodded and continued down the hall, as if she didn't have the energy to deal with him. "I'll let her know."

"That was strange," Echo said, watching the woman walk away.

"Very." Rand hadn't had a lot of contact with the staff, beyond Morton and Dumont, but he had seen this nurse around the clinic before. And though she might be pretty and young, she'd never seemed anything but perfectly professional.

Turning his attention back to Vanderhoven, Rand led the way to the room marked with the lab tech's name. Inside, Vanderhoven was reclining in his bed as before. This time, instead of *Star Trek,* the television hummed with what had to be the music from a porn movie.

Rand glanced up at the television. Sure enough, bodies tangled on the screen. Thankfully, it seemed to be more nudity and kissing, rather than the hard stuff. Rand shifted his feet on the floor, overly conscious of the fact that Echo was standing next to him.

When he looked back to Vanderhoven, a knowing smile lifted the corners of the lab technician's pale lips. "Detective McClellan, are you feeling better?"

He could just imagine what Vanderhoven thought of him after yesterday's visit. "I'm fine. How are you feeling?"

"Stronger. More awake. Dr. Morton adjusted my medication. He said I should be able to think more clearly."

Oh, *that* was what he was doing. Thinking. Rand raised a skeptical brow at the TV. "Glad to hear it. Then you'll be able to answer a few more questions. Turn this off, and we can get started."

Vanderhoven ignored the request, instead turning his pale-blue eyes on Echo. His smart-ass expression morphed into a smile of clear sexual interest. No doubt he would like to see her starring in his entertainment of choice. "I think you need to introduce me first."

Annoyance pricked Rand's skin. "This is Echo. Echo Sloane."

Vanderhoven raised his nearly invisible blond brows. "Are you related to Brayden Sloane?"

"He's my brother."

"What a relief." His smile widened. "I thought you were going to say he was your husband."

Rand fought to keep from rolling his eyes. A smooth operator Vanderhoven was not. "Let's talk about Bray Sloane."

"I can't tell you much. Macho military types don't hang out at the same lunch table with geeks like me. That's one thing that hasn't changed since high school. But some women are attracted to a brilliant mind, aren't they, Echo?"

"Mr. Vanderhoven, I—"

Keeping his eyes on Echo, Vanderhoven nodded to the television. "You've got to see this, Echo. It's the best part."

On the screen, a woman gathered each side of her blouse in her hands and pulled, popping buttons into the air and baring her breasts.

Out of the corner of his eye, Rand saw

Echo look away from the screen and focus on him.

He almost groaned. Even though he hadn't suffered a breakdown like that last time he was here, this interview was still turning out every bit as bad as he'd imagined. Only, in his worst-case scenario, he was the only one humiliated. Not Echo, too. "Turn that off, Vanderhoven. Now."

Vanderhoven didn't seem to hear him. Instead, he stared at Echo's breasts. "I'll bet you'd be great at that."

Anger rose in Rand like a soaring temperature. He didn't know what he'd do first, turn off the TV or shove his fist through the skinny geek's face. He stepped toward the bed.

Echo grabbed his arm. "Wait."

Heat pulsed through Rand's suit coat where her fingers grasped his sleeve. Even her touch was soft. Gentle. He could imagine her fingers on his bare skin. Moving across his chest, down over his belly. Her featherlight caress arousing him.

Hardening him. Until she reached lower and took him in her hand.

His pants grew tight.

What in the hell was he thinking? What was he doing, fantasizing about sex when he was supposed to be questioning a witness?

And more important, how could he stop?

It was happening again. The same thing that had happened yesterday. But instead of fear, instead of depression and the wish for death, lust had claimed his mind. His lust for Echo Sloane.

Please, don't let her notice. Please, let her be looking somewhere else.

He glanced at her.

Her eyes were averted, but she wasn't looking somewhere else. She was staring straight at his crotch. She moved her gaze up his body and met his eyes. "You feel it, too. Don't you?"

Her voice was barely more than a whisper, but it kindled inside him like a flame. Building. Growing.

She searched his eyes. Tilting her head back, she parted her lips.

He stepped close and lifted a hand to touch her hair. Silken strands sifting through his fingers, he pushed it back from that incredible, heart-shaped face. He needed to kiss her, learn what she tasted like, learn how she felt. Not able to resist a moment longer, he lowered his mouth to hers.

She tasted sweeter than he could have imagined, and he couldn't get enough. He wrapped his arms around her, pulling her body tight to his, tangling his tongue with hers, devouring her like a starving man.

This couldn't be happening. He must be out of his mind. Dreaming. Hallucinating. He'd been attracted to Echo since he met her. To her body, of course. Any man would be. But even more to the fierce determination that made that soft body come alive.

But attraction was normal. Something he could keep in check. That wasn't what he felt now. Now he was obsessed beyond reason. He had to have her.

A moan rose in his throat. He cupped her breast, kneading the softness, feeling her nipple harden and press against the confinement of her bra. His body trembled with the need to remove her clothes, to caress her naked skin.

This was insanity. Desire he couldn't control. He couldn't stop. He had to take her. Right here. Right now. He couldn't live unless he buried himself inside her.

He couldn't live.

"Oh, man, this is better than any movie."

Hell. Vanderhoven was watching, staring at them from his bed. Rand couldn't tell if he was affected too. Maybe that was why he was watching porn. Maybe that was why he was egging them on now. Maybe there was something in the air in this room, an experiment of Dr. Morton's. But whatever Vanderhoven was feeling or Morton was up to, Rand didn't care. He could think of only one thing. And he had to get Echo away from him before he totally lost control.

He grabbed her arms, pulling her hands off him. "Echo, you've got to go."

"I need you. Right now." Confusion streaked across her face, followed by hurt.

Hurt that he'd caused. He gritted his teeth. "No."

"But you want me, too. Don't you want me, too?"

More than she could know. "Get out. Now." He steered her toward the door.

Her back straightened, rigid.

"Go." Please.

She marched for the door without looking back, passionate anger in each abrupt sway of her hips.

God help him.

She closed the door with a slam.

Rand shut his eyes and struggled to keep himself from following. He wanted to catch up to her, take her into a vacant room, give in to the heat surging through his body. Dragging in a deep breath, he turned to face Vanderhoven.

"Sloane's sister sure is a hot little number," Vanderhoven said. "Although I wish you would have at least undressed her before you pushed her out."

What Rand wouldn't give to knock the smile off Vanderhoven's face. Anger buzzed through him, almost as hard to control as his lust for Echo. Gritting his teeth, he strode to the television and yanked the cord from the wall.

"Hey, you have no right to do that."

"No more games, Vanderhoven. You're going to tell me what you know about Bray Sloane, and you're going to tell me now."

"I have no problem telling you anything you want to know about Bray Sloane. Believe me, after what he's put me through, I'm not about to protect him."

Rand's gut hitched. "What are you trying to say?"

"Bray Sloane set off the explosion. He nearly killed me and his partner." He folded his hands behind his head.

"What makes you think that?"

"I don't think it. I know it. I heard him talking about it. On his cell phone."

"When?"

"After the explosion. He thought I was unconscious. He thought I didn't hear. He was wrong. I heard every word."

The muscles in Rand's neck cramped

until he wasn't sure he could turn his head. He'd come here to get the full story from Vanderhoven, and now he didn't want to believe it. He didn't want it to be true. "What did he say?"

"That he wanted his money."

"And you're sure he was talking about the explosion?"

"I'm sure."

"Do you have any idea where he went after that?"

Vanderhoven shook his head. "I must have passed out. When I woke up, I was here puking my guts out and having those damn dreams. But you might want to go out there and ask his sister."

"Why is that?"

"Because before I lost consciousness, I heard him making another call. And I heard him say her name."

Chapter Five

"Whatever Wesley Vanderhoven thought he heard, he's wrong. He misunderstood." Echo marched down the sidewalk outside the Beech Grove Clinic. She knew it had been a mistake letting Detective McClellan kick her out of Vanderhoven's room before she'd gotten her answers. If she hadn't been so muddled, so confused, so…carried away, she never would have let it happen.

Her cheeks heated with thoughts of how she'd kissed him. She'd never gotten so carried away in her life. Especially with some guy she didn't even know, let alone trust. And not only had she embarrassed herself, she'd blown her whole reason for going to Beech Grove.

"He remembers very clearly what your brother said. He also remembers Bray making another call. And saying your name."

She stopped in her tracks and turned to face him. "Why would he say my name?"

"You tell me."

His implication dawned on her. "You think *I* talked to Bray after the explosion? You think I know where he is?"

"Vanderhoven seems to think so."

"He's wrong. If I knew where Bray was, do you really think I'd file a missing person's report? Do you really think I would have spent over a week worried out of my mind?"

"I can pull your brother's cell phone records. I can see who he called."

"Then do it. You'll see. He didn't call anyone to demand his money, and he didn't call me." She didn't know what else to say. It seemed the more she denied it, the more guilty she looked. "I don't see why you're taking Vanderhoven's word about this. The man was the victim of a chemical explosion. He's in a mental institution."

"He might not be the ideal witness, but that doesn't mean he can't remember at least some of what happened."

She thought about Vanderhoven's strange lascivious comments. From the time she stepped in the door, he'd been out to get her, out to humiliate her. "Or maybe he's just angry about what happened to him. Maybe it's just easy for him to blame it on Bray, since he's not here to defend himself."

"Maybe."

The word might imply he was open-minded, but judging by his tone of voice, he'd already tried, convicted and sentenced Bray.

And there was nothing she could do about it.

RAND GROUND HIS TEETH together as he followed Echo across the parking lot to her car. Their discussion about her brother had gone about as well as he'd feared. Not only had she refused to believe a word Vanderhoven said, judging by the abrupt swing of her hips, she was angry.

Really angry.

Just about the worst state of mind for her to be in for what he needed to ask. "Echo, wait."

She kept walking, heading for a piece-of-junk car that looked as if it had seen better days. "I'm sorry, Detective," she tossed over her shoulder. "I can't stomach any more of your accusations against my brother. I've had plenty for one morning."

"It's not about your brother."

Reaching the car, she slid her key in the lock, opened the door and climbed inside.

He slipped between the open door and the car frame. Crouching, he blocked her from closing him out. "I need to talk to you."

"We already talked. Now, if you'll excuse me, I have to stop for diapers on the way home, and my babysitter has an after-noon class."

"This will only take a second." He might be crazy for bringing up what had happened in Beech Grove, or he might just be crazy. Whatever the case, he had to know if she felt the strange emotional effects in Vanderhoven's room, too. He had to know if there was something strange going on at Beech Grove, or if he really did need that appointment with the shrink he'd set for this afternoon. "Please."

She let out a sigh. "Okay. What is it?"

He looked into her big gray eyes. Now that he had her attention, how in the hell was he supposed to ask without seeming like a lunatic—even if that was what he was? "Did you feel something happen in there?"

"Something? Like what?"

Was she really not sure what he was talking about? Even now all he could think about was their kiss. Of being so caught up in the press of her body against his that he couldn't focus on anything else. "You really don't know?"

A crease formed between her eyebrows. "You're talking about our kiss, aren't you?"

"Yes. Did you feel it?" he asked again. "That your emotions were getting away from you. That they were too strong to control."

Her frown softened, ever so slightly. But she held her lips tight, as if she was reluctant to trust him with what she had to say.

How could he blame her? "Did you feel anything like that? I really have to know." He sounded as though he was coming on to her, but he didn't know how else to ask. He didn't want to tell her what he suspected. Especially since he had no way of knowing if it was anything but wishful thinking on his part.

"Is that what you felt? That you couldn't control yourself?"

A heavy feeling sank into his gut. "You didn't?"

She gave him a troubled look that he didn't know how to read. "Yeah, I guess."

Not exactly what he was after. For him the feeling had been so strong, there had been nothing else. The way he burned to touch her. The ache to plunge inside. It had taken over every part of him. There was no guessing involved.

She narrowed her eyes to gray slits. "What is this really about? If you think this is going to make me tell you I know where Bray is, you're nuts. I don't know."

So that was what she thought of him. That he'd try to seduce her in order to get her to turn in her brother? "I told you, this is not about your brother."

"And why should I believe that?"

He shook his head. He had no reasons to give her, no reasons she'd buy. "For the last time, I'm not trying to blame your brother. I'm trying to find the truth."

She stared at him unblinking.

He was obviously not going to get any of the answers he needed until he came clean with her. Or at least as clean as he dared. "A cop was killed at Cranesbrook Associates yesterday. A cop I knew."

"And you think Bray did it?" She shook her head, as if she'd never heard something so stupid in her life.

"I don't know who did it. But this mess involving Cranesbrook and Beech Grove isn't going to end until I find out who's behind it."

"It's not Bray."

"Maybe not. Maybe you're right. But even if he's not guilty of anything, it's just as important that I find him. He could be a witness."

She nodded, as if she just might accept this answer. "So what does that have to do with what I may have felt in Vanderhoven's room?"

He didn't know. His suspicions might be nothing more than wishful thinking. "I need to understand it."

"What's to understand? People are attracted to each other. People even have sex."

So she was attracted? "That wasn't normal attraction, Echo. Not what I felt. It was so strong, it was like being insane."

The troubled look returned to her eyes. "Listen, I ended a relationship not too long ago. Or rather, he ended it. And after being abandoned by the father of my baby, I don't have the stomach for any kind of attraction. Normal or not."

She didn't understand. She must not have felt what he had. Maybe it was all in his head. A product of stress and lack of sleep. A mental breakdown. "The last thing I want is a relationship, Echo. That's not why I was asking."

"Well, there you go." She gripped the steering wheel with both hands and stared through the windshield. "I'm glad we got this all settled. Now I have to go, if you don't mind."

He forced his cramping legs to straighten and stepped back from the car, allowing her to slam the door.

She leaned forward, turning the key in the ignition. The engine clicked, but didn't fire. She turned the key again. Face pink, she slammed her hands on the wheel.

He shouldn't get any more involved with Echo Sloane. She had a cell phone. She could call a tow truck. She didn't need him. But somehow he couldn't make himself believe that. He couldn't walk away. Just seeing that frustrated pinch to her mouth made him want to protect her. Fix things for her. Put a smile on those lips.

He grabbed the handle and opened her door. "I'll give you a ride."

"HERE, LET ME carry it for you."

"No problem." Gripping the grocery bag filled with diapers and teething crackers, she thrust herself out of the passenger seat of Rand's sedan and walked past his outstretched arms. She had planned to do a bigger grocery shopping, but wandering through the aisles with the detective on her heels had made that impossible. She couldn't even remember what she needed, let alone organize herself enough to find it in the store. She just wanted to get home. Get away from him.

And she sure as heck didn't want him to step foot inside her home. Being around him while she was feeling so raw and vulnerable—and *attracted*—was a trick too cruel to be believed.

She ran up the steps to her tiny house without looking back, unlocked the door and slipped inside. Blowing out a breath she hadn't been aware she was holding, she closed the door behind her and leaned against it.

The low sound of a woman weeping caught her ear. "Shanna?"

No answer. Only more crying.

Echo peered in the direction of the sound, the dark hallway leading back to Zoe and her bedrooms. Had something happened to the babysitter? Had something happened to Zoe? Her heartbeat launched into double time. She scurried into the hall, willing her eyes to adjust to the dim light. "Shanna? What's wrong?"

Shanna curled on the floor along the wall. Her crying wobbled, but Echo couldn't decipher the words.

Echo fell to her knees beside the young woman. "Shanna? What's wrong? Are you hurt?"

"Oh, God," Shanna forced out between sobs.

Echo smoothed the girl's hair back from her damp cheek. "Slow down. Try to breathe."

"I…couldn't…stop…him."

"What?"

"He's…" She choked out a sputtering cough. "In…her…room."

Echo raised her gaze to the door at the end of the hall. *Zoe's room.* Was someone inside? A man? "Who, Shanna? Who's in Zoe's room?"

The girl hiccupped. "I…don't…know."

Down the hall, the door opened. A man's head peered out—his face covered by a black ski mask and dark sunglasses.

He held Zoe in his arms.

A wave washed over Echo. Fear, desperation and incredible anger. She scrambled to her feet. "Give me my daughter!"

The man didn't say a word, didn't take a step. He merely stared at her.

She couldn't breathe. She couldn't think. Balling her hands into fists, she launched herself down the hall. "Give me my daughter!"

He shot out a fist, clipping her jaw.

She slammed against the wall. Her head spun. She clung to the wall, keeping herself standing with willpower alone.

He pushed past her, jabbing an elbow into her back as he went by.

Pain ripped down her spine, but she willed herself to stay on her feet.

He stepped over Shanna without stopping, without looking.

Shanna's body tightened into a ball. Sobs shrieked from her lips.

The man strode for the door. Zoe's wails rose from his arms. As if she knew he was taking her. As if she knew she'd never see her mommy again.

Echo forced her mind to clear, to focus. She couldn't let him leave the house. She couldn't let him take her baby.

She pushed herself away from the wall and staggered forward. Fear blinded her. Desperation filled her throat, as hot as the taste of blood. Focusing the swirl of emotion to a point—a point centered on Zoe—she pushed on.

As if in slow motion he grabbed the doorknob and pulled the door open. Light pierced the dark room. His silhouette slipped through the doorway, stepped onto the stoop.

She got to the door. She had to stop him. Reaching through the opening, she grasped the arm of his black trench coat and she held on.

He pulled his arm back, tearing the fabric from her grip. Then he yanked the door closed, pinching her arm against the jamb.

She pulled the knob, but his grip was too strong. She thrashed her hand, beating at a face she couldn't see. A scream ripped from her throat. If only the detective was still outside. If only he would hear.

The door released and she stumbled backward. Recovering her balance, she plunged out onto the stoop.

A fist slammed into her jaw.

Her head snapped back. The blow rang through her ears; color swirled behind her eyes. She could feel herself sinking to the ground. She could sense him moving away, down the steps, across the yard. Stealing her baby. Stealing her life.

She willed herself to her feet. Willed them to carry her down the stairs. Her head throbbed and spun. Her arm ached, but she pushed on. But even before she reached the ground, she knew she couldn't catch him. She knew he was gone.

pushed on. But even before she reached the ground, she knew, she cut into it once more.

She knew he was gone.

Chapter Six

A scream cut through the small town like a siren.

Rand whipped his car around and raced back in the direction of Echo's house. It was Echo. He knew it, even though for the life of him, he didn't know how.

As soon as he turned the corner onto her street, he saw her stumbling across the lawn. "Stop him. Please. You have to help me stop him."

He had no idea what "him" she was talking about, but it didn't matter. He snapped open his holster and pulled out his weapon. He caught up to her just as she stumbled, almost going down. He grasped her arm, holding her up. "What happened? Are you okay?"

"He took Zoe. Hurry!"

"Who took Zoe?"

"I don't know. But you have to stop him. That way!" She pointed through a hedge.

He glanced back at his car. He'd have to run. He'd never have time to circle the block in his car and catch a running man before he made it through the yards.

He raced for the hedge. Sharp branches of boxwood clawed at his suit, catching and holding. He yanked it free, the fabric ripping. Up ahead, he spotted a figure dressed in black, wearing a ski mask.

And clutching Echo's baby in one arm.

Rand pushed his legs to move faster. His breath rasped in his ears. The grass skimmed slick beneath his shoes.

He could see Zoe's arms flailing. Hear her screaming. The man stopped and stared at him, as if he no longer had the need to run.

Rand felt the gun ready in his hand. He couldn't shoot from this distance, and certainly not while running. He couldn't risk a miss. He couldn't risk hitting Zoe. He had to be careful.

Careful.

His stride faltered and slowed. A feeling of caution swept over him, so strong he almost stopped.

What was wrong with him? He'd always run toward danger. Toward gunshots. But now the need for caution overwhelmed him. It was all he could do to keep it from bringing him to his knees.

It was happening again. The overwhelming emotions. Yet this time he wasn't in Beech Grove. This time he was out in the fresh air.

He bit his lip, hoping the pain would bring him control as it had before. The taste of copper filled his mouth but the fear kept building, fear that he would do something to hurt Zoe. Hurt a scared little baby.

The man turned and resumed running.

Rand forced himself to follow. He couldn't lose the man. If he did, Zoe would be lost, as well.

Another bout of fear ripped through him

followed by the hollowness of failure. He pushed on. The emotions weren't real. They couldn't be. There had to be some kind of explanation.

The man disappeared into the yard of one of the large homes that flanked the river.

Rand raced on. With the man gone, the powerful swirl of emotion started to fade. He picked up his pace, racing along the path the man had taken just as a boat engine growled to life on the water below.

A speedboat raced out onto the river, moving fast. The man looked up at him, and with the last glance came a wave of despair that drove cold into the marrow of Rand's bones.

"EVERY COP IN THE STATE will be on alert. We'll find her, Echo." Rand knelt in front of her and gathered her hands in his. He'd gotten her back in the house, planted her on the couch and checked on the still-sniffling babysitter before he'd called dispatch. Soon the place would be swarming with cops. Cops who would find Zoe.

He could only hope.

"What happened? How did he get away?"

Rand felt sick deep in the pit of his stomach. He had the same questions. Questions he couldn't answer. "He stole a boat," he said simply.

She buried her face in her hands. "It's all my fault."

"*Your* fault?"

She shook her head. Her flinch of pain was visible even though she still covered her face. "If I had been able to hold him longer, he wouldn't have had such a big head start. You could have caught up to him."

An old ache hollowed out in his chest. He couldn't let her blame herself. Not when it was his fault.

He smoothed a hand over her hair. "You did everything you could."

"It wasn't enough."

"But it wasn't your fault. If this was anyone's fault, it was mine."

"Yours?" She looked up at him as if what he was saying didn't make sense.

Maybe it didn't to her. He only wished

he was as lucky. "I've been experiencing some strange things. Things I can't control. Emotional reactions."

"Does this have something to do with what you were talking about outside of Beech Grove?"

"Yes. I thought maybe it was caused by something. That it wasn't just in my head."

Echo shook her head. "It wasn't just in your head. I felt it, too."

Rand took a slow breath. He'd been desperate to believe he wasn't going crazy, that the emotional surges were coming from outside him. But now he was almost afraid to ask. "What did you feel?"

"I was attracted to you all along. But in Vanderhoven's room, I suddenly couldn't control myself. It was like a switch being thrown. I couldn't *not* touch you. I couldn't *not* kiss you."

He nodded. He'd felt the same way. As if he couldn't stop his mindless desire.

"I just figured that I was so tired, I wasn't thinking right. That lack of sleep wore away my inhibitions, I guess."

"But now you think it was more than that?"

She nodded.

If they had both felt the overpowering emotion, it had to be caused by an outside influence. But there was still a piece missing. "But you weren't overwhelmed with emotion when Zoe was stolen?"

"He had my baby. He was taking her." Her voice trembled as she let out a shuddering breath. "I'm not sure what I felt. Scared, angry, desperate to get her back. The feelings were strong, out of control, but they seemed…"

"Normal under the circumstances?"

"Yes. But…"

He leaned forward. "What?"

"Shanna." Echo glanced at the hall toward the master bedroom where the girl had gone to lie down. "When I walked in, she was lying in the hall, curled into the fetal position. She was sobbing so hard she couldn't talk."

The man hadn't hit the girl. Rand had checked her for injuries himself. She'd been shaken up, frightened, but physically she'd been fine. "It could have been just plain fear. That has got to be scary for a teenager. She's what, eighteen?"

"Nineteen. I suppose it would be awfully scary. Still it was strange, you know? He was still in the house, just a few feet down the hall in Zoe's room, and she was just lying there crying. Not running. Just crying like her heart was broken."

He would definitely have a talk with the babysitter when she was up to it. Find out exactly what she felt.

Memory niggled at the back of his mind. The St. Stephens cop, Woodard. When Maxie had been killed, state troopers had found Woodard in the hall. He'd been crying. Could it be related? Could Maxie's killer be the same man who'd kidnapped Zoe?

Still one thing didn't fit the pattern. One thing didn't make sense. "If something is out there that can amplify emotions, and if the man who took Zoe used it on Shanna and me, why didn't he use it on you?"

He didn't expect her to answer. There

was no answer. At least, not one they could find knowing as little as they still did.

"What do you think could cause something like that? A drug?"

"Who knows? Maybe. Something administered through the air." He thought of his first theory, back when he was scrambling to explain to himself how he wasn't having a mental breakdown. "Maybe something being developed at Cranesbrook. And tested at Beech Grove."

"You really think so?"

He shook his head. "I don't know what to think."

"Can you find out? Search the place? Find out if someone at one of those places took Zoe?" She stared at him with desperate eyes.

"We've searched Beech Grove, top to bottom."

"How about Cranesbrook?"

"We have an evidence team combing it now. At least, everything we can get warrants for." The truth was their search was limited. And unless he could prove to a court that the scope of the search should be widened, they wouldn't even scratch the surface of a place like Cranesbrook. "But the reality is, we don't know this has anything to do with Cranesbrook. We don't even know what we're searching for."

She let out a long, shaky breath.

For a moment he thought she would cry. Instead she raised her chin and sat up straight, as if forcing all her willpower into her spine.

She was some kind of woman. He hated to think how he would react to losing a child. One reason he'd never entertained having one. "We'll find Zoe, Echo."

"How?"

"There are things we can do. Bloodhounds are on the way. Sometimes they can pick up scents even on the water. And we can put out an Amber Alert, use the media to help. The FBI has Rapid Start and Evidence Response Teams that we've called in to assist. We'll find her, Echo. We'll pull out all the stops."

"But if the man who took her can control

emotions, what are the chances that anyone will be able to get her back?"

He opened his mouth to give her an answer, then closed it without saying a word. He didn't know the chances. He didn't have a clue what they were up against. He wasn't sure he dared try to explain it to anyone.

Anyone but Echo.

She looked up at him, her eyes puffy, her beautiful face drawn and taut. "Thank you, Detective."

"Call me Rand." He laid a hand on hers, tracing over her soft skin with a fingertip. He shouldn't have given her his first name. He shouldn't be touching her now. He was coming dangerously close to getting personally involved. But somehow he couldn't stop himself.

She needed him. And he couldn't turn his back. Even though turning his back was exactly what he had to do. For her sake. And for his own.

MOLLY BAKERHOF CUDDLED the little baby girl in her arms and hummed the soft lullaby she'd honed to perfection in the years of raising her own children and grandchildren. This little girl was a gift. Molly's arms had ached with emptiness in the years since her youngest grandbaby had grown too old for holding. But now that ache was gone and the sweet smell of baby shampoo swirled around her like the most precious perfume.

She'd been so lonely since dear Fred had died. This little apartment had seemed small when he was alive. Now it was too big. Her life too quiet. She'd been so bored lately, she'd even contemplated getting a television.

But all that had changed. With this sweet child in her arms, she didn't need the new fall season of reality shows and crime dramas.

She was sorry the baby's mother was going through such problems. Severe depression was not to be taken lightly. But at least Molly could be a help. She'd make sure the baby was safe and loved until the mother could work through her problems. Until she could return to her child.

"However long it takes, I'm here, little one. Gramma Molly is here."

ECHO'S HAND SHOOK as she picked her most recent photos of Zoe from her computer's printer tray. State police and FBI scoured the neighborhood and combed every inch of her tiny home and yard. They'd taken her fingerprints as well as Shanna's and had covered nearly every surface of Zoe's yellow room with fine black powder in an effort to capture the kidnapper's fingerprints.

Rand hadn't been exaggerating when he'd promised to pull out all the stops on the investigation. Already she'd talked to so many officers and FBI agents that she could no longer tell them apart.

"Are those the pictures?" Rand crossed the living room and held out a hand.

She gave him the photos. She pointed to one in which Zoe wore a pair of stretchy yellow pants and a top sprinkled with bears. "She was wearing this outfit."

He nodded. "I'll get these pictures circulating right away."

Tears swamped her eyes once again. She couldn't control it. Whenever she thought of her little girl out there, maybe cold, maybe hungry, without her mommy to keep her safe…

Rand handed her a tissue.

She took it, swiping at her eyes. "I'm sorry."

"No need."

She shook her head. "I'm not very good at controlling my emotions sometimes."

"And you think now's the time that you're going to start?" He gave her a gentle smile.

Just the kind of smile she needed. When she'd first met Rand, she'd been convinced he was the most emotionless man she'd ever met. She didn't think that anymore. He was reserved, certainly. Tightly controlled. But there was definitely a tender, protective side to him.

The side that had helped her get through the last few hours. "Have you found anything?"

"We have blockades set up along all highways leaving town. We're putting a tap on your phone. With the FBI involved, their Evidence Response Team and Rapid Start Team should speed up analysis of any evidence he left behind as well as helping us check out every lead we can come up with as quickly as possible. The blood-hounds arrived a few minutes ago."

She'd seen the dogs through the front window. "Do you really think they can follow Zoe's scent across water?"

"Bloodhounds have miraculous noses. If there's a scent out there to get, they'll get it."

She dragged a breath into her lungs. She might not be feeling better—that would only happen once she had Zoe back in her arms—but she was feeling more hopeful. "Thanks."

"You don't have to thank me, Echo. It's my job."

Maybe so. But the way he'd smiled at her, the gentle way he explained all that was going on...she couldn't help think there was something more.

Or maybe she just needed something

more right now. Someone she could trust. "What about the Amber Alert?"

Rand gestured to the stack of photographs and description of Zoe's clothing that he'd had her write out. "That's partly what this is for. She'll also be listed with the National Center for Missing and Exploited Children. And we already have a bulletin out to law enforcement agencies all around the Chesapeake Bay area. We'll find her, Echo. We'll get her back."

Her legs trembled, with relief, with hope, or just plain fear for Zoe, she didn't know. She lowered herself onto the couch and grasped her thighs with her hands. "I hate feeling so out of control. Like I can't *do* anything."

"You are doing something, even though it doesn't feel like it. Answering questions, providing photos, that's a lot, Echo."

The trill of the phone ripped through the living room.

Echo stared at the cordless receiver lying on the coffee table. A wave of heat washed over her, followed by chilling cold. "Do you think it's him? Do you think it's the kidnapper?"

"It could be." Rand waved an arm to an officer across the room. "Do we have a trap-and-trace on this phone yet?"

The officer shook his head.

"I have Caller ID." Echo said, her mind finally clicking.

"That will have to do." Rand nodded to the phone. "Go ahead."

She picked up the phone, trying hard to keep her hand from shaking. Taking a deep breath, she turned it on and held it to her ear, tilting the handset out so Rand could listen. "Hello?"

Rand sat on the couch next to Echo. He leaned toward her, his ear close to the phone.

"I don't want to hurt the baby." The voice sounded strange, electronically altered.

Echo gripped the phone hard enough to make the plastic casing creak. "I'll do whatever you want."

"I don't want anything from you. I want your brother."

"Bray?"

"Tell him to meet me."

"I don't know where he is."

The caller's breathing rasped in her ear, but he said nothing.

Her throat constricted. Did he believe her? What was he thinking? What was he going to do? "Please."

"Find your brother, because I'll only give the baby to him."

The line went dead.

"What's the number?" Rand barked to an FBI agent.

Echo held her breath. If they had a number, they could trace it to the caller, couldn't they? They could find Zoe.

"Looks like a cell phone."

Rand let out a breath.

Echo searched his face. "What? They got a number, isn't that good?"

"I'm betting it's a disposable cell. Anyone who is careful enough to disguise his voice is careful enough not to call on his own cell. But we'll be sure to check it out."

Tears surged again, but she blinked them

back. She set the phone on the table and gripped her thighs. "He wants Bray. Why?"

"I was afraid of this."

"Afraid of what?"

"Whatever your brother has gotten himself into, now you're being dragged in along with him."

She would never believe Bray did something illegal that caused this to happen. He was a victim, maybe a witness, but that was it. Still, Rand was right about one thing. She was involved. Zoe was involved. And somehow Echo had to figure out how to get more than Bray out of this mess now. "What am I going to do?"

Rand touched a cool finger to her chin and guided her to face him. "You're going to make those lists of names and addresses. I'm going to find your brother. And your baby. You just have to trust me."

HE COULDN'T STAND the idea of the pain she must be going through. He only wished he could make it easier. Or save her from it altogether. But all he could do was his best. And the way things were going, his best was woefully short of good enough.

He'd already told Echo about the dogs losing Zoe's scent on the water. And she'd faced the lack of fingerprints with a stiff upper lip. What he didn't want to tell her was that the roadblocks and neighborhood canvas hadn't turned up anything yet, either.

And now...he looked back down at the report in his hand, the debrief with Officer Woodard from the St. Stephens Police Department. In it, he mentioned a wave of strong emotion, an urge to cry. But he'd attributed it to his mother's recent illness.

But the worst of it was Rand couldn't get more information from him. He couldn't talk to him about his experience. In what the St. Stephens PD assumed was a fit of grief and guilt over Maxie's death, Officer Woodard had hanged himself this afternoon. He'd been swept away by emotion once again, and only Rand understood what that meant.

Whoever had killed Maxie had taken another victim. And he was likely the same man who had stolen Echo's sweet little child. The same man who was after Bray Sloane.

The whole thing revolved around Project Cypress, Cranesbrook Associates and Beech Grove. And if Rand was going to have a shot at keeping his promise to Echo, he had to start there.

Checking to make sure that Echo was concentrating on her list-making and not on him, he approached one of the dark-suited FBI agents. Unease shifted in Rand's gut. He never liked to share too much with the feds. Especially when they could be so damn stingy with sharing the information under their control. But since he didn't have any other avenues opening before him, he was going to have to take some risks. "Hey, Freemont."

Based at the district office in Baltimore, Jim Freemont had turned out to be a decent guy on previous cases. Decent enough that he might just do Rand a little favor, considering the circumstances.

Sipping at coffee with so much cream it

was lighter than his skin tone, Jim nodded. "Rough case."

"Especially since it dovetails with another rough case we've been wrestling with."

"Oh? What case is that?"

"Echo's brother, Brayden Sloane, disappeared after an explosion at a chemical research facility in the area. Place called Cranesbrook Associates."

"The same brother named as ransom for the baby?"

"The same. We have reason to believe the explosion wasn't an accident."

Freemont waited for Rand to go on.

"They were working on something called Project Cypress in the lab where the explosion took place. It might help if someone could nose around, sniff out what Project Cypress was or who it was for."

"It's a contract with Washington?"

Rand shrugged. "Cranesbrook often does work for Washington."

"You might be out of luck, then. I'm assuming it's pretty hush-hush if you haven't figured out what it is already."

Rand gave a nod.

Freemont shook his head. "Even if I ask the right questions, I can only get so many answers."

"I know the chances are slim. But Zoe Sloane's chances are getting slimmer with each hour that passes. Anything you can find out could help. If I could get an idea of what the purpose is behind the project, I might be able to find out who the players are."

"And who is trying to smoke out Sloane?"

"Right."

Freemont glanced at Echo, then gave a reluctant nod. "I have a pretty good nose. Let me make a few calls."

"I appreciate it." Rand slapped Freemont on the shoulder and headed for the door. While Freemont was sniffing out information about Cranesbrook, he was going to try to solidify the Cranesbrook-Beech Grove connection. He had an appointment to keep with a psychiatrist.

Not the one who was expecting him.

Chapter Seven

Echo knew she was supposed to be too distraught to notice, but when Rand slipped out the door, she was right on his heels. "Where are you going?"

"I'm checking up on some leads."

"I'll go with you."

He raised his brows, as if she'd just said the most outrageous thing he'd heard in his life. "Not necessary."

"I need to do something to find Zoe, Rand. If I sit here any longer, I'm going to go crazy."

"You've done a lot. And you have more to do. Things you need to do here at home."

"What?"

"Answering questions. Giving us names

and addresses of anyone who was interested in Zoe. Just generally being available. Only you can do those things."

Frustration stormed her nerves. The feeling of being out of control. A feeling she'd hated since she was a child. "I've already given you everything I have."

"You might recall more. People, circumstances—things that might have a bearing on the case that you didn't remember at first."

"I can tell you if I think of anything."

"What if the kidnapper calls back?"

Her stomach quivered at the thought. She would never forget that creepy, electronically altered voice. The voice of the bastard that took her Zoe. "Do you think he will call back?"

He looked away from her. "Never know."

"You don't think he will any more than I do. Not yet, anyway. Besides, I have my cell phone with me. I can forward my calls."

He blew a breath through tight lips, the stream of air misting slightly in the cool evening.

"You can't think of any other reasons I can't go, can you?"

"I'm working on it."

"I feel so helpless sitting here. I can't find Zoe. I can't help Bray." She shook her head. She had to make him understand how doing nothing was eating her up. "It reminds me of when I was a kid. When Bray and I used to sit by the window and watch for Dad to come home. Only day after day passed, and he never came."

"I'm sorry. Darnell told me your father left, but not how."

"He just went out one day and never came back. And no matter how hard I wished he would, no matter how long Bray and I waited, it made no difference." She looked out at the street. Houses lined the other side, their shadows growing impossibly deep and dark as the sun slipped below the horizon. "All I can think about is Zoe being out there somewhere. Cold. Hungry. Scared. And I can't warm her and feed her. I can't hold her and sing her songs and tell her everything is going to be okay.

I can't even tell myself that. At least, I can't believe it."

Lines dug into Rand's forehead. "Driving around with me isn't going to change any of that."

"It'll make me feel better. It'll make me feel like I'm doing something to find her."

He let out a heavy sigh. Striding to his blue sedan, he opened the passenger door. "We're just making one stop. Who knows, maybe you'll be able to bring more pressure to bear on this guy than I've managed so far."

It didn't take long for Rand to drive them to a little restaurant along the water by the name of Moncelli's Seafood and Steak. Echo had heard wonderful things about the place, though since even McDonald's was a strain on her budget, she never dined at a place this fancy. The dining room lived up to its reputation. Candlelight and linen, fresh flowers and the most elegantly dressed diners. She felt out of place as soon as she stepped inside.

Of course that would never stop her.

"Table for two, sir?"

Rand waved off the host. "We're not staying. Just delivering a message to one of your diners." He stepped forward into the open dining room and strode for a table occupied by a short man with thinning blond hair. Judging from the crème de menthe on the rocks in his hand and the snifter across the table, he and a companion had reached dessert.

"Hello, Doctor."

Dr. Morton's eyes bugged for a second before he reasserted control. "Detective." He glanced at Echo.

"This is Echo Sloane."

Morton nodded. Recognition or just politeness, Echo couldn't tell.

Rand pulled out a chair for Echo and folded into one himself. "Where were you at around eleven this morning, Doctor?"

Morton snorted a derisive laugh. "I've already explained my whereabouts to your Detective Farrell about an hour ago. Maybe you should demand he share his notes."

"I know you talked to Farrell. Who do you think told me where I could find you?"

Echo looked from Dr. Morton to Rand. If Morton had already been questioned by police, what did Rand hope to accomplish by talking to him again?

"This is harassment."

"Answer the question."

"I was sailing on the Chesapeake. I have a rock-solid alibi. I did not kidnap some baby."

Echo thrust out her chin. "Not some baby. My baby."

He arched bushy blond brows. "I didn't know. I'm sorry. But I don't have any idea where your baby is, miss. I can't help you. Now, if the two of you don't mind, I've answered enough questions for one meal."

"Kidnapping is a major felony. Did you know that if that baby is taken across state lines, it becomes a federal case? Not that we waited for that to happen before we requested the assistance of the FBI."

"Why are you telling me this?"

"Are you conducting experiments on the residents of Beech Grove?"

"What?"

"You heard the question, Doctor."

"I just can't believe what I heard."

"Maybe you'd like to take a trip to the state police barracks and give me a chance to fully explain it to you."

Morton glanced up as if looking for his dining companion. "I've heard all I need to hear."

"But you haven't answered the question."

"No. We're not conducting experiments on our residents. I resent you even implying something like that."

"I've heard from a reliable source that there have been some strange emotional phenomena—"

"Let me guess, Gage Darnell told you that." He leaned forward, keeping his voice low in an obvious attempt to prevent the surrounding diners from hearing. "Mr. Darnell came to us in a paranoid condition. He was disoriented, violent. He kept ripping the IV from his hand. We only secured him so he wouldn't hurt himself. He was never a prisoner. And he was never experimented on."

"There is evidence—"

"Evidence? Except for what Gage Darnell thought he experienced, you have no evidence. You've turned our clinic upside down, and you've found nothing. And if you don't leave me alone, I'm going to have my lawyer file a suit against you for harassment." He leaned back in his chair and crossed his arms over his chest. "I'm done talking."

Echo glanced at Rand. Why didn't he say something about his own experience? Or hers? Why didn't he back Morton against a wall? "That same emotional phenomenon was used when my baby was kidnapped."

Morton narrowed his eyes on her. "Really? Do you have details?"

Rand stared at her.

She wasn't sure if he shook his head or not, but she wasn't about to stop either way. Now that she'd gotten Morton's attention, she wanted some answers about Zoe. And she didn't plan to return to her living room until she'd accomplished something toward finding her daughter. That was why she was here. "When I walked in the door, my babysitter was lying on the floor, sobbing. She was so distraught, she could hardly tell me that a man was in my daughter's room only feet away."

"The experience sounds very upsetting. Why do you think that response was abnormal or had anything to do with Beech Grove?"

"Because Rand and I both felt similar things there."

Rand shot to his feet. "We have to go."

"Similar things? Can you describe your feelings?" The doctor clutched his glass and leaned toward her over the table.

"Echo," Rand said in a low voice. "Now."

She looked at Rand and then back to Dr. Morton. Why did he want to leave so badly? Couldn't he see they hadn't gotten any answers yet?

"Trust me," he said.

She let out a long breath, feeling Rand's eyes drill into her. Trust him. Easier said than done.

But in the last few hours, he'd been there for her. Trying to get Zoe back. Trying to help her cope. He'd even agreed to take her on this interview with him, something he didn't have to do. She supposed the least she could do was give him the benefit of the doubt....

As long as he explained himself before they reached the car.

RAND HAD NEVER BEEN more grateful to see someone get up from a table. Here he'd been worried about Echo becoming upset, not being able to handle the pressure of talking to Morton after losing her baby just hours before. Echo Sloane might be soft and sweet on the outside, but she had a frame of steel underneath. He should have spent more time explaining the situation to her and less time worrying.

Rand looked down on Dr. Morton. "I'll tell my supervisor to expect your complaint. And, Morton?"

He didn't answer.

"If I find anything at all connecting you

to the kidnapping, I'll give you some fuel for those harassment charges. You thought your clinic was turned upside down before, you ain't seen nothing yet." Nodding to Echo, he led her toward the exit.

She stopped just on the other side of the hostess stand. "What's going on? He might have told us something if you hadn't cut the interview short."

"I didn't come here to tell him everything we suspect."

"But I thought you wanted answers. I thought you wanted to find out what Morton knew about the emotional amplification."

"I wanted him to worry about what we knew, that we were able to tie it to the kidnapping."

"Well, now he has something to worry about."

"No, now he knows we're going on nothing but our own feelings. Feelings aren't evidence."

"Oh." She let out a shaky breath. "I'm sorry. I just wanted answers so badly. Did I blow it?"

Across the dining room, an impeccably groomed man with dark, parted hair and expensive shoes wove through tables. Martin Kelso smiled at a waitress, his dark eyes crinkling at the corners.

Rand watched him stop at Morton's table, slip into a seat and pick up his brandy snifter. By stopping here in the entrance, Echo had given him the answer to a very important question. "No, you didn't blow it."

Echo followed his gaze. "Who is he?"

"Martin Kelso, acting president of Cranesbrook Associates. The question is, why is he having dinner with Morton? And why didn't they want us to know about it?"

RAND FOUND Special Agent Freemont as soon as he and Echo walked in the door. If he could find out what Project Cypress was or at least whom it was for, maybe he could determine what the dinner between Kelso and Morton meant.

He glanced at Echo. Freemont would never talk in front of her. "Find out anything?"

He shook his head. "No calls. But then, we didn't expect another one."

Next to Rand, Echo sucked in a shaky breath.

Rand touched her elbow. "Can you excuse us for a second? We have some other business to discuss."

She searched his eyes, no doubt trying to figure out what other business he could possibly have that was so important. Finally she nodded and walked down the hall to the bedrooms.

Rand let out a breath. He knew Echo didn't trust anyone. At least, no one but her brother. She'd obviously been put through the wringer in the past. But in the last few hours, it seemed she'd started to trust him. The last thing he wanted to do was let her down.

He focused on Freemont. "How did your sniffing go?"

"I talked to my contact. He directed me to a friend in the DOD."

The Department of Defense? Rand's

pulse started knocking double time. "So Project Cypress is a weapon."

"I didn't say that. In fact, I didn't say anything about this matter. Not a single word."

The speed of Rand's pulse bumped up to triple time. "Did you hear anything about a Dr. Morton or the Beech Grove Clinic doing testing for Cranesbrook?"

"Morton? Don't know him. But I doubt he has the security clearance needed to breathe the same air as someone involved in this project."

"How about on the side? Without the DOD's knowledge?"

Freemont shook his head. "No way. Cranesbrook management would have to be crazy to take a chance like that. This is big-time stuff."

Rand nodded. Morton might not have a connection that easy to find, but Rand knew it was there. "Is this thing big enough to kill to keep it quiet?"

Freemont gave a short nod.

"What does Project Cypress do?"

Freemont smiled as if he'd caught Rand trying to slip by a fast one. "I told you, McClellan. I can't talk about it, even if I knew."

"Is it an emotional agent of some sort? Something that amplifies human emotion? Drives the enemy out of their minds?"

"I've told you all I know."

"Come on, Freemont," Rand urged. He hated to pressure the guy to step out on a limb he obviously worried would break. But this was important. Life and death. "You said you'd try to help."

"And I tried. That's all I can do."

Damn the tight-lipped federal government. Rand had dealt with it before. But he'd never been as frustrated as he was now.

Still, it wasn't Freemont who was stonewalling. Rand knew that. He'd probably revealed more than he should. "I appreciate you checking for me."

Freemont nodded. "If I were you, I'd be quiet about this. And careful."

A phone rang, cutting through the ominous rumble of Freemont's warning.

Rand's cell. He flipped it open. "McClellan." Rand could feel Echo's eyes on him from across the room.

"I need you at the barracks." Nick's voice.

"Why? What happened?"

"I'll fill you in when you get here. Until then, you might want to watch what you say to the FBI. And to Echo Sloane."

RAND FOUND NICK in his office. The usually laid-back bear of a man paced the aisles between the cubicles that housed the detectives' desks and files, as fidgety and nervous as a high-strung horse. "You didn't show up at your psychologist appointment today."

"You can't be all worked up over that."

"You gave me your word. I vouched for you with the state's attorney, and you didn't come through on your end."

"Give the state's attorney my apologies. You might want to mention something about a kidnapped baby." He let the sarcasm slide thickly off his tongue. "Now, what is this really about?"

"Want to sit?"

Rand's gut tensed. "No."

Nick heaved a deep breath. "The lieutenant got a call from the FBI."

"And?"

"They're taking over the investigation of the Cranesbrook accident."

It's a good thing he didn't take a chair. Hearing that would have shot him out of it like a damn spring. "Why?"

"You know the FBI. They throw around 'interstate this' and 'federal law that,' but all it means is they want the case."

"But what about Maxie Wallace's homicide?" Not to mention Officer Woodard.

Nick pressed his lips into a line.

"They're taking that, too? They can't."

"They can. You're the one who tied it to the lab explosion. They're claiming jurisdiction over anything tied to Cranesbrook."

"Oh, hell."

"I'm not any happier about this than you are." Nick paused, letting his sentence hang in the air as if it was only half-finished.

"What else?" Wait a minute. Rand could

guess. "They're going to look into my shooting of Edmonston."

Nick nodded. "They've asked for a copy of your files."

Could this get any worse? He thought back to what Nick had said on the phone. He hadn't only mentioned the FBI. "What about Echo Sloane? Why was I supposed to watch what I said around her?"

"We're going public with the search for her brother."

"You're what?"

"You heard me. We're releasing his name and picture in conjunction with the Amber Alert for Zoe Sloane."

"He didn't take the baby."

Nick held up a hand. "I agree it's doubtful he kidnapped his niece. But the ransom request is only part of the reason to step up the search, get the public to assist us."

"What's the rest?"

"Follow me." He led Rand down the hall to the conference room.

Hank Riddell stood as they entered. Sandy

hair mussed and glasses smudged, the research fellow looked as if he'd just pulled an all-nighter in the lab. "Hello, Detective."

"Hank says he has proof that Brayden Sloane caused the accident at Cranesbrook," Nick explained.

Rand raised his brows in Nick's direction. Apparently, Nick waited to share this bit of information with him before he turned the whole thing over to the feds. "Let's hear it."

A knock sounded on the door.

Nick pulled it open. "Yes?"

A trooper stood outside. "Detective Sergeant? There's someone from the FBI here to see you."

"Show him to my office." Nick's gaze dug into Rand. "Handle this. Quickly."

"Sure thing." When the door closed behind Nick, Rand turned back to Riddell. "What do you have for me?"

Riddell pulled a thin jewel case from his coat pocket and extended it to Rand. "It's from surveillance cameras we have set up in case of emergency in one of the labs."

Rand studied the disk. With no label or

other means of identification, he'd have to watch it to know if what Riddell said was true. "From Lab 7?"

Riddell nodded.

"Why didn't you turn this over before?"

"I just found it."

Good try. "An officer found a DVD from the Lab 7 camera in Sid Edmonston's office yesterday. This wouldn't be it, by chance?"

Riddell shook his head. "Sid must have made his own copy. That must be what your officer found. This is the original."

"How can you tell?"

"The time stamp and date on the video."

This was fishy. More than fishy. Not only had Riddell made it difficult to find him in the past when Rand and Richard had questions about the murder of the janitor at Beech Grove, but he hadn't been very forthcoming when they finally had tracked him down. "So what made you bring this forward now? You haven't been the model of co-operation in the past."

"I didn't have anything to tell you in the past. I can't talk about Project Cypress.

That hasn't changed. And I told you the truth about what I was doing in the Beech Grove Clinic. Wes and I are friends. I was watching out for him and the company. I've done nothing but cooperate as much as I could." He adjusted his glasses with a shaking hand. "When I found this in archives, I figured I could finally do something to help but still not lose my job."

Rand pictured the meticulous acting-president of Cranesbrook enjoying a snifter of cognac with Dr. Morton. "Does Martin Kelso know you're turning this over to the police?"

"I…I don't know."

"Does anyone know?"

"Dr. Ulrich gave me the go-ahead. He's my supervisor. I'm sure he checked it out with Kelso."

Riddell might be sure Ulrich cleared it with Kelso, but Rand wasn't. As Edmonston's replacement, Kelso might very well want to hide the truth as much as his predecessor.

Slipping on latex gloves, Rand took the

case from Riddell's hand and plucked the disk from it. Now it was clear why Nick had the research fellow waiting in the conference room. Equipped with television, DVD player and DVD recorder, the room would be ideal to check out this particular bit of evidence before turning it over to the FBI.

Slipping the DVD into the player, he hit the record button on the unit underneath and turned on the television. An image flickered to life on the screen. An empty lab.

"See along the bottom?" Riddell pointed to a black band running under the image. The time, date and lab number were branded in red. "That's the day of the accident. And the time is an hour before the alarm went off."

"You said the camera is there to record emergencies. If this is an hour before, there's no emergency yet."

"That's not how it works. The cameras are constantly recording, but the images are recorded over every forty-eight hours.

When an alarm sounds, the images are flagged and all the footage is preserved."

"You have this feature in all the labs at Cranesbrook?"

"All the labs that are in operation. We have some labs not in use. No reason to monitor those."

It made sense. But Rand still wasn't about to buy into Riddell's sudden cooperative act. "Why would Edmonston make a copy of something he wanted to cover up?"

"I would only be guessing."

"Then guess."

"It would be a good way to keep Sloane in line in case he decided blackmail might be a good way to make even more money."

"Sloane?" Rand shoved away the image of Echo's concerned eyes. He couldn't worry about her feelings. He had to pursue the evidence no matter where it took him. "How does Sloane fit into this?"

Riddell nodded at the television. "Watch."

For another minute Rand stared at an empty lab, until a shadow appeared on the screen. A man followed, tall as Rand but with a body that spent many hours in a weight room. As he strode toward the chemical storeroom, his spiked black hair glistened in the overhead lights. He pulled the door open. Pausing, he looked over his shoulder toward the camera, as if checking to make sure he wasn't watched. It was Sloane, all right. Rand might never have met the man, but he looked just like his photo.

And his eyes were the same shade of gray as Echo's.

Once Sloane disappeared inside the storeroom, Riddell turned to Rand. "Sloane was a security expert. He had no business messing around with lab equipment. And he really had no business in that storeroom."

Rand knew Riddell's answer before he asked the question. But he had to ask, anyway. "That was the same chemical storeroom where the explosion took place?"

"Yes. Less than an hour later."

He checked his watch. He didn't know how long Nick could hold off the feds, but he hoped it was long enough. "You said the cameras record continuously, right? I want to see the explosion."

Riddell shook his head. "You can't see much, with the smoke and all. The camera kind of malfunctioned."

A loud knock sounded on the door. Without waiting for an answer, a man pushed into the conference room. He wore a dark suit so polished and bland he could only be FBI. "Detective McClellan?"

Rand's gut seized. "Special Agent…"

The man didn't offer a name. "The FBI is taking over this investigation, including that recording. And I expect you to turn over all your notes pertaining to Cranesbrook Associates to your supervisor by noon tomorrow."

Chapter Eight

Echo stared openmouthed at the headline in the morning paper, anger ringing in her ears: Security Expert Sought for Questioning. The headline might seem innocuous, but the article itself definitely suggested the police were interested in more than merely questioning Bray.

The sound of a car door slamming came from outside.

Echo scrambled up from the kitchen table, raced to the door and pulled it open just as Rand mounted the steps. She shoved the paper against his chest. "What is this?"

He didn't even glance down. "We have to find your brother immediately. You know that better than anyone. The public might be able to help."

"This makes Bray look like a wanted criminal."

"It says he's wanted for questioning. He is."

"'Wanted for questioning about the explosion and his niece's kidnapping'? It's bad enough that you're accusing him of blowing up a lab where he was in charge of security. This sounds like you think he kidnapped Zoe, too."

"The article didn't accuse him of anything."

"It might as well have. That's the message it sends." A horrible thought popped into her mind. "You don't really *believe* Bray kidnapped Zoe, do you?"

"No."

"How about the explosion?"

"You know I've always had questions about that."

"He didn't have anything to do with it. He wouldn't."

"Echo, I saw him."

"What?" He couldn't have said what she thought she heard.

"We found the lab surveillance video. Bray is on it."

"On it? How?" If Bray was on that video, it was because he was caught in the explosion, hurt, maybe killed. As difficult as it was to swallow those possibilities, if that was what happened to her brother, she'd have to accept it. But she would never accept Bray was responsible. That just wasn't possible.

"I have something you need to see." He crossed the living room and knelt in front of the armoire that held the television and DVD player Steven had been forgetful enough to leave behind. Turning on the machines, he pulled a disk from his pocket and slipped it in.

The image of a laboratory flickered on the screen. A man walked into the lab and strode to a supply room. The image was grainy, but she could clearly recognize her brother's face. "He isn't doing whatever you think he's doing."

Rand pointed to the bottom margin of the picture. "This was recorded in Lab 7 an hour before the explosion."

She shook her head. It couldn't be right. It didn't *feel* right.

"Echo, the explosion came from that storeroom."

Tears blurred her vision. She wiped them away with the back of her hand. "You can't even tell what he's doing in there. It could have nothing to do with what you're saying."

"What is a security contractor doing in a chemical storeroom? There are no security systems in there. He has no business in there."

She shook her head. She didn't care. She wouldn't believe it. Not about Bray. "How did you get this video? Where did you find it?"

"A research fellow at Cranesbrook turned it over to us last night."

"He must have faked it."

"Echo…"

"You don't think it's strange that a

research fellow suddenly discovers this? After all this time?"

"I had reservations at first."

"What changed?"

"I ran it by a video expert this morning. He said from what he could tell, it looked authentic."

"From what he could tell. My point exactly. He could be wrong."

He pressed his lips together, as if trying to keep himself from breaking the bad news.

"He could be, Rand."

"We have to proceed as if he's not."

The threat of more tears stung her sinuses. "You mean as if Bray is guilty."

"I have to follow the evidence, Echo. If Bray isn't responsible, he's going to have to give me some reason to believe it. So far everything I have points to his guilt."

"If he was here, he would give you plenty of reason."

"That's my point exactly. Why isn't he here?"

"Missing doesn't mean guilty. He could be hurt." She swallowed, trying to fight back the tightness in her throat. "He could be dead."

Rand closed the distance between them. Raising his hand, he lightly touched her arm, as if trying to make her feel better, taking care of her as he had after Zoe was kidnapped.

She fought to keep the tears in check. "I know collecting evidence is your job, Rand. But evidence doesn't always tell the whole story."

He lowered his hand. "It's the only story that matters. I have to go by the evidence in front of me."

She forced a nod. "And I have to go by what's in my heart." Strange how just last night she'd let herself believe she could trust Rand. Now everything had changed. The trust starting to form between them had turned to awkward pain. "I suppose you've ransacked Bray's house by now."

He gave her a sideways look. "Actually, no."

"What stopped you?"

"The small matter of a search warrant.

Until that surveillance video, I didn't have enough evidence against him to give me probable cause to search his home."

"So what stopped you after you got that video?"

"The FBI has taken over everything having to do with Cranesbrook."

"What does that mean?"

"That if your brother caused that explosion, he's going to be in trouble with the feds not me."

The nervous tension in her stomach turned to nausea. If the FBI believed Bray caused the explosion, they might also have decided he was a terrorist. Who knew what would happen to him then?

And it wasn't just Bray.

She rubbed her forehead with her fingertips. Her head was throbbing, her heart aching. "If Bray is thrown in prison, he won't be able to help get Zoe back. What will happen to her?"

Rand nodded. "*We* need to find him first."

She scanned the kitchen, her gaze landing on her purse. Grabbing the vinyl strap, she swung it over her shoulder and started for the door. "Are you coming?"

"Where?"

"Bray's house. I'll prove to you that my brother isn't hiding anything. And maybe you'll find something I didn't see—something that will tell us where he is."

It didn't take long to make the drive to Bray's house along beautiful Turtle Creek. Rand parked behind Bray's black Corvette and they walked to the door. She slipped her key in the lock of the ranch-style brick home and pushed inside.

"Front door open," a vaguely electronic female voice said.

Echo stepped into the small foyer area. Finding the security panel, she punched in the code to deactivate the security system.

"Nice system," Rand said, entering behind her.

Echo nodded and scanned the open floor plan. Bray's house looked just as she'd left it the last time she'd come looking for information about where her brother might have gone when he fell off the face of the earth.

The clean, masculine lines, the rough-hewn furniture said it was a man's home.

She paused as she passed the table displaying the framed photo of her holding Zoe. He'd snapped the photo in Zoe's room, right after Echo had finished decorating it with white ruffled curtains and yellow walls with multicolor balloons sprinkling the wallpaper border. Bray had been so proud of all she'd done with the house, so in awe of his little niece, seemingly more at ease than usual. And she looked happy in the picture, too, holding her baby, smiling at the pride in her brother's eyes.

She *was* happy.

Swallowing the thickness in her throat, she led Rand to the dock where Bray kept his laptop computer. She opened it and turned it on. Slipping into the chair, she tried not to notice as Rand moved close and peered over her shoulder at the screen. Logging on to Bray's e-mail program, she started scanning his mail.

"How do you know his password?" Rand asked, his deep voice humming in her ear.

"He gave it to me when I was on bed rest here the weeks before Zoe's birth. He said he might need me to check his e-mail for him when he was at work. Really, I think he just wanted to keep me from feeling so helpless." It had worked, and now she was repaying his kindness by searching through his things.

She pushed that uneasy thought from her mind. Better that she and Rand look through his files than the FBI. Besides, Bray had nothing to hide. She'd stake her life on that.

She clicked through e-mail after e-mail. Business e-mails from Gage and Five Star's manager, Peggy Olson. Personal notes from her. And, of course, the usual spam. She glanced up at Rand. "See? Nothing remotely suspicious."

"Unless he destroyed the suspicious ones," Rand said. "I would have."

Echo shot him a look. She clicked out of Bray's e-mail.

"How about his finances?"

She shrugged a shoulder, as if his

enduring skepticism didn't bother her in the least. She clicked on the icon for Bray's money management program. "I told you, Bray is very successful. He even helps me with my money."

Out of the corner of her eye, she could see him crook his brow. "Really? How?"

"When I was pregnant with Zoe, I suffered some complications my meager health insurance policy didn't even begin to cover. That and the time I had to take off from work depleted the down payment I'd saved to buy my little house. Bray not only lent me money for the down payment, he helped me organize my healthcare debts so I can afford to pay them off a little at a time. If not for him, I would have had to declare bankruptcy, and I would have lost the house." She let a bitter laugh escape her lips. "With the bankruptcy laws the way they are now, I never would have been able to dig myself out."

"He sounds like a great guy."

She wasn't sure if he was being sarcastic or sincere. "He *is* a great guy. That's why he never would have sabotaged a client's business. Not for money. Not for any reason." She opened the list of Bray's accounts and their balances.

Red numbers stared back at her.

She shook her head. This couldn't be right. It couldn't be.

Rand leaned close to the screen. "It looks like this place is mortgaged to the hilt. He also has taken out a personal loan and depleted any savings he might have had."

"I don't believe it. He would have told me if he had money problems." Echo's mind swirled. "He would have told me."

Rand took over the computer, clicking into the accounts.

The numbers stared at her in glaring detail. She thought she was going to be sick.

"He wrote a couple of huge checks to a hospital."

She nodded. "My medical bills." She wrapped her arms around her middle. He hadn't reorganized her debts; he'd paid them.

"And this check to you."

"My house down payment." Tears

swamped her eyes, turning the computer screen into a blur. "Why did he lie to me? Why didn't he tell me he couldn't afford to help?"

"He probably knew you wouldn't take his help if you knew the truth."

She thought of how hard Bray drove himself. Was that for her? So he could pay off her bills? She couldn't believe it. She didn't want to. "He always took care of me, when we were kids, I mean."

"After your father left?"

She dashed the tears off her cheeks with the back of a hand and looked up at Rand. "Yeah. And Steven."

"Zoe's father?"

She managed a nod. "Steven didn't want to be a dad." It still hurt to say it. To even think it. Even though her feelings for Steven were dead, she doubted the pain of his betrayal and rejection of Zoe would ever go away.

"You've got to be kidding."

"He didn't want the responsibility."

"Sorry." Rand's voice sounded rough.

Full of emotion she'd never heard coming from him.

A tremble started at the base of her throat. She looked up into his dark eyes. Eyes so concerned…and so in pain. She couldn't speak.

The slam of car doors came from the front of the house.

Rand straightened and started for the door.

Echo scrambled to follow. She caught up to Rand at the entrance.

Men in dark suits strode up the sidewalk toward them.

"Who are they?" she whispered, even though she knew.

Rand's jaw hardened. "FBI."

Chapter Nine

Rand watched the FBI agents circle the black Corvette and approach the house, the muscles at the back of his neck stiffening the closer they came.

The lead agent pulled a document from the jacket of his dark suit and offered it to Rand. "We have a federal warrant to search the premises."

Rand took the paper. He didn't need to look at it. He knew it would be in order. And that it would include everything in the house and car, including the laptop that he'd barely started poking through. "So you guys are getting warrants now?"

The special agent shook his head. "Great. A comedian."

Rand knew he should keep his smart-ass jabs to himself. But he was so damn frustrated that the feds picked this exact second to show up, he was lucky he could conjure up a businesslike tone.

He glanced at Echo, pushing from his mind the thoughts of her painful confession. Truth was, he was relieved the moment with Echo was cut short. The thought of some unfeeling bastard hurting her like that was too close to home. Too close to the fears skirting on the edge of his own mind. Fears of hurting her, disappointing her.

Fears that seemed to grow closer the more evidence against Sloane he found.

He focused on the warrant. So spelled out. So clear. What had him angry was letting Sloane's laptop fall into FBI hands. A few more minutes and he might have found something. A few more minutes and he could have some real answers, instead of guesses. A few more minutes and he might have either proved Sloane's innocence…or his guilt.

Either way, things would be settled.

"What does it say?" Echo asked.

He handed her the warrant.

She studied the document, her face pinched with a troubled frown. The paper rattled in her shaking hand.

The agent gave her a polite smile. "It would probably be easier if you didn't stay."

She shook her head. "I have to reset the alarm."

Rand touched her arm. He could feel her tremble even through her jacket. "You've been through a lot, Echo. You don't need to see them go through your brother's house."

"But I have to make sure..."

"They'll lock up. I'll bring you back later to reset the alarm." He slipped his arm around her shoulder.

Her body fit against his just the way it should. He couldn't ignore the protective feeling coursing through him. As if just by holding her he'd become bigger, stronger, invincible.

God help him.

"Come on." He escorted her out of the

house, past the agents searching the black Corvette and to his car. Opening the door, he guided her inside and climbed behind the wheel. The sooner they could get out of here, the better.

"I can't believe it." Echo's voice barely rose above a whisper.

He started the engine and backed out of the drive. He wasn't sure if she was talking about the FBI searching her brother's house or what they'd found on his computer. "I'm sorry things are happening this way, Echo."

"He's in debt because of me."

"You can't blame yourself. He made his own choices."

Her gaze snapped to him. "Just because Bray is in debt, doesn't mean he caused the lab explosion."

He nearly groaned. He didn't want to have this conversation with her. Her allegiance to her brother was blind, deaf and dumb. "I'm getting the idea that no amount of evidence is going to convince you."

She looked down at her hands, folded in

her lap. "Bray is the only person who has ever stuck by me. He's the only one I ever felt I could trust. If I can't trust him, I don't know what to believe in anymore. Do you know what I mean?"

He knew. He knew all too well. "You believe in facts. In my experience, people will let you down every time. Facts don't."

"That sounds like a lonely way to live."

She had no idea. Truth was, neither had he...until he met Echo Sloane.

The bleat of his cell phone cut through his thoughts.

Echo's gaze snapped to him, her body nearly vibrating with tension.

He flipped the phone open and held it to his ear. "McClellan."

"Your court order came through." Nick's voice boomed in his ear.

He shook his head, letting Echo know it wasn't about Zoe. Turning away from her, he walked into the living room, trying to get straight in his mind what Nick had said. "You're talking about the court order for Vanderhoven?"

"You're free to get him out of there. It seems once the judge got an eyeful of Gage Darnell's affidavit, he wasn't willing to take the chance the same thing was happening to Vanderhoven. A couple of troopers are on their way to assist."

"Thanks, Nick."

"Let's wrap this up before the feds decide Beech Grove and Vanderhoven belong to them as well."

"Will do." He clapped the phone shut.

"What's going on?" Echo asked. "Did someone find something?"

"It wasn't about Zoe. I'm sorry."

She slumped back against the seat. "So what was it?"

"Vanderhoven. I'm going to bust him out of the nuthouse, and get him away from whatever-the-hell Morton is up to." He hesitated, waiting for her to demand to go along the way she had last night. The way she had the time they'd tried to question Vanderhoven together. "I have to do this alone."

She nodded, the bob of her head abrupt.

"Drop me off at the shop where I work, then. Maritime Lullaby."

"You're going to work?"

"I can't sit home and wait. At least at the shop I can do something."

She'd been desperate to do something last night, anything that would make her feel less helpless. And at least if she was at the gift shop where she worked, she wouldn't be with him. "All right. I'll pick you up when it's over."

RAND PULLED OPEN the front door of the Beech Grove Clinic and led the troopers inside. He wasn't sure what he'd find, but dealing with whatever emotional tricks Morton had up his sleeve would be easier than dealing with the *real* emotions Echo inspired.

Of course, then there was Vanderhoven. The last time he'd talked to the lab tech, he'd acted more like a lab rat unwilling to leave his cage. Hopefully he'd be as easy to convince of the danger as the judge had been.

Dr. Morton and Nurse Dumont met

them in the entrance as if they'd been waiting. "What is going on here?" Morton demanded.

"I have a court order to remove Wesley Vanderhoven from your facility." Rand handed Morton the document advising him of the order.

Morton let the paper fall. It skimmed along the shiny waxed floor. "Mr. Vanderhoven has no interest in leaving."

"If you'll study that paper you just dropped, you'll find the court is concerned that Mr. Vanderhoven isn't capable of determining what is in his best interest right now. Not while he's under your influence."

"Are you still harboring that delusion about experimentation going on here? Really, Detective. What movies have you been watching? You must learn to separate fact from fiction."

"The court order speaks for itself."

"This court order is bull." Morton's scalp shone red through his thin blond hair.

"Take that up with the judge. Now please, step to the side."

Morton dug a roll of mints from his lab coat and opened it with shaking hands. He popped one into his mouth like he was popping Valium, then stepped toward the office door.

Nurse Dumont gave Rand a sharp look then glanced at Morton. Surprise streaked across her harsh features. "Doctor?"

"There's no way to hide it anymore, nurse. If the detective wants to go to Mr. Vanderhoven's room, take him there."

The nurse spun like a cadet and marched down the hall. When she reached Vanderhoven's room, she stepped to the side, giving Rand and the state troopers free access.

Rand stepped inside and focused on the empty bed. Great. "All right, Nurse Dumont. Where is Wesley Vanderhoven?"

"It seems he left."

"Left? He just walked out?"

"Yes. So you see, your charges that we're holding him here are ridiculous."

"Unless you and Dr. Morton were stalling us at the entrance so other personnel could remove him."

The nurse issued him a hard, condescending glare over the wire rims of her glasses. "I assure you that's not the case."

"At this moment, your assurances aren't worth much."

One side of her mouth twitched in what some might call a smile. "Go ahead. Ask the rest of the staff. The patient was gone before breakfast this morning. And it isn't the first time. Wesley Vanderhoven has left before."

Chapter Ten

Rand drove down Beech Grove's long winding drive with a weight on his shoulders that would cripple an ox. A warning look from Morton, and Nurse Dumont had developed acute amnesia about the specific dates and time that Vanderhoven had gone missing from the clinic, but that didn't keep Rand's imagination from taking over where she'd left off.

Reaching the intersection with the highway, Rand pulled to the side of the road and punched the state police barracks' number into his cell. A transfer later, and Nick's voice came over the line. "Detective Sergeant Johnson."

"Vanderhoven isn't at Beech Grove."

"McClellan? Something just came in. Hold on."

The two state troopers' cars passed him and turned onto the highway. Finally, Nick came back on the line. "Vanderhoven just drove out the gate at Cranesbrook."

Cranesbrook. The pressure on Rand's shoulders grew. Every time he'd felt the emotional amplification, Vanderhoven had been present. Every time *except* Zoe's kidnapping. Unless the morning the baby was kidnapped was one of those times Vanderhoven had chosen to leave the mental hospital.

Unless Vanderhoven had been the man in the ski mask.

Rand pulled out onto the highway and stomped on the gas. "Where is he now?"

"A St. Stephens patrol officer is following him. He's heading into town."

Funny. Rand hadn't heard anything on his radio. "Does St. Stephens PD dispatch have their repeater off?" Without the repeater sending out the signals to all police radios, the communication between dispatch and the pursuing patrol car went only two ways.

"We're keeping this to ourselves right now. No need to have the FBI swoop in and take Vanderhoven away until we can find out what he knows about Beech Grove and, of course, Cranesbrook."

Rand smiled. State or local, police took the brotherhood—and sisterhood—of blue seriously. The FBI might want to keep the local law from knowing what was going on in their investigation, but that didn't mean state and local police were going to step aside willingly. Not when two of their own had died.

Rand wasn't the only one who wanted justice for Richard and Maxie. "I'm heading downtown."

"Wait, McClellan. Hold on. I have another call from St. Stephens."

Rand held his breath.

Time ticked by so slowly, he was tempted to take off before Nick's voice came back over the phone. "Vanderhoven's driving a blue Passat that belongs to one of the nurses at Beech Grove. He has just parked on Waverly Street and is entering one of the shops."

"Waverly Street?" Rand took a left off the highway and onto the road leading into the heart of St. Stephens.

"You know it?"

"Yeah. What shop?"

"A place called Maritime Lullaby."

Rand's gut seized. "Gotta go, Nick. Hear anything else, you let me know."

He clapped the phone shut and focused on driving. Vanderhoven hadn't picked that shop for its unique knick-knacks, that much was certain. Somehow, he had found out Echo was there. And if his theories about Vanderhoven's absences from Beech Grove were correct…

It didn't take long to wind through the narrow streets lined with quaint shops and city parks that looked like they'd emerged straight from a long-ago past. He spotted the white-and-pastels sign of Maritime Lullaby from a block away. And in front was parked a blue Passat.

He swung to the curb, stopped behind the car and jumped out. Down the block he spotted the St. Stephens cruiser. Motioning to the cop at the wheel, he crossed the red cobblestone sidewalk, raced up the shop's wooden stairs and pushed through the door.

The jingle of the shop bell rose over the pulse of blood in his ears. He stepped inside.

A large display of hand-painted wooden ducks and lighthouse lamps dominated the shop's main room. Smaller shelves bearing maritime-themed toys and children's bedroom decor filled the room nearly to bursting.

He could see no sign of life, let alone a skinny blond scarecrow. Or Echo. "Vanderhoven?"

Shoes scuffed the wood floor behind a rack of woven blankets bearing seafaring scenes.

"Come out where I can see you."

"What do you want, McClellan?"

"We have to talk."

"You wanted me to leave Beech Grove? Well, I left."

"I don't have a problem with that." Rand peered toward the back of the shop. Was Echo safely in the back room with her price stickers? Or was she among the shelves of stuffed neon-orange crabs next to those blankets that still hid Vanderhoven? "I want to talk about Morton, about what he's doing."

"We've already covered that."

"I was hoping that you'd have a little more to say now that you're not under his control."

Vanderhoven stepped out from behind the blankets. His face looked more gaunt than the day Rand had first talked to him at Beech Grove, his neck and shoulders skinny as a skeleton. "I was never under Morton's control."

The pressure pinched Rand's neck. He stepped closer, slowly rounding the light-houses. Vanderhoven was playing some kind of game, that was clear. But what it was, Rand couldn't yet say.

Right now, in addition to convincing the lab tech to talk, he wanted to see Vanderhoven's hands. Make sure he didn't have a weapon. Make sure he wasn't a danger to himself or anyone else. "Why did you leave Beech Grove? The last time we talked, you were perfectly content there."

"It's not for the reasons you think."

"You know about it, don't you? The emotional amplification? You've felt it."

The side of Vanderhoven's lips quirked up in a smirk. "No, but you have."

The door to the back of the shop swung open. "Rand? What's going on?"

He turned to meet Echo's surprised gray eyes. "Wes and I were just talking. I didn't mean to distract you from your work." He stared at Echo, willing her to disappear back into the storeroom, back where she'd be safe.

Her gaze flicked to Vanderhoven. "What are you doing here?"

"I…need to find your brother."

"I don't know where he is."

"Now, why don't I believe that?"

Rand stepped around the lighthouses and circled a bin filled with pillows in the shapes of shells. "If you want to find Bray Sloane, I'm the one you want to talk to, not Echo."

"Rand?" Echo started toward him.

He held up a hand. He wasn't sure why he got the feeling that Vanderhoven was dangerous. He had no evidence of that fact. Nothing more than the strange way the lab tech was acting. The strange way he'd acted before. But alarm blasted over his nerves like a siren, and he wasn't going to take the chance the feeling wasn't right. Not with Echo in the room. "Come outside with me and we'll talk about Sloane." The alarm blared louder, ringing in his ears, making his head throb.

Vanderhoven shook his head. "I'd rather talk to her. Not only do I doubt you have any idea where Sloane is, but she's prettier." He smiled at Echo, if you could call open leering a smile.

Jealousy gripped low in Rand's gut. Jealousy he had no right and no reason to feel. "You stay away from her."

Vanderhoven stared at him. "You know, women don't like it when you get too jealous."

Rand put a hand on one of the nearby

shelves to balance himself. He *was* jealous, damn it. The emotion twisted and writhed inside him like a snake. He wanted to grab Echo, drag her outside, keep her all to himself. And if he couldn't have her—

The rickety wooden shelf shifted under his weight. A dozen toy fishing boats dumped to the floor.

"Oh!" Echo lunged for the shelf. Falling to her knees, she started picking up the toys.

Rand struggled to get a grip. It was happening again. The emotional surge. The insanity. He had to get out of here. But before he did, he had to make sure Echo was safe. "Echo." Her name wrenched from his throat.

Echo focused on him, her eyes wide and confused, her lips pinched and her eyebrows dipped. "You broke them."

"What's going on?" a voice shrilled from the back room. An older woman rushed into the store. "Oh my God, what happened?"

Rand scrambled, his feet skidding on plastic. He wanted to punch Vanderhoven, beg Echo's forgiveness, throw her over his shoulder and haul her to safety all at the same time.

It had to be Vanderhoven. He had to be causing it.

Rand bit his lip, forcing his mind to clear if only for a second.

Vanderhoven stared at them with those eerie pale-blue eyes. His face was set in a mask, as if he didn't feel anything at all. As if he wasn't affected.

"You're doing this." Anger and fear surged over Rand. He couldn't breathe. He couldn't think. It was as if he was drowning in emotion.

Still crouched on the floor over the broken boats, Echo started to sob.

The strangled sound of her crying ripped through him.

Echo had to get out. And it was up to Rand to make sure she did. Dipping low, he grabbed her around the waist and lifted her, tossing her over his shoulder in a squirming, awkward move.

Her crying erupted in a scream. Her fists

landed on his back. "Let me down. What the hell do you think you're doing?"

"I'm saving you. I can't let you get hurt." Holding her legs fast, he raced for the door, hitting two more shelves on the way. The shop owner yelled as they burst outside and thundered down the wooden steps.

The St. Stephens cop met them at the sidewalk. "Detective, what's going on?"

The damn question of the day.

He wanted to tell the guy to run, to get out while he could. He couldn't find the words. Emotions clanged in his head, writhing and wrenching, tearing him apart.

"Let me go!" Echo yelled, struggling and scratching like an angry cat. "I have to go back in! Joyce is in there!"

The shop door slammed.

Rand looked up the stairs and into the hypnotic eyes of Wesley Vanderhoven.

The cop groaned. He groped blindly at the snap on his holster, then fell to his knees.

On the street, tires squealed. Metal smacked metal. Car doors flew open and angry voices screamed obscenities.

Rand had to stop it. He had to prevent innocent people from getting hurt. But he couldn't move. He couldn't think.

Vanderhoven walked slowly down the steps. He was the only sane person on the street. The only one not affected.

Because *he* was causing the insanity.

The only way to make it stop was to stop *him*.

Rand reached for his Glock. His fingers touched the grip.

Ringing rose in Rand's ears. Sound clanged through his head. Beside him, the officer was crying, tears rolling down his face. Echo struggled in his arms, trying to race up the stairs to reach the woman in the store. And all Rand could do was hold her tight.

He couldn't protect St. Stephens. He couldn't protect Echo. Who the hell was he kidding? He couldn't even protect himself.

Chapter Eleven

An hour had passed since all hell broke loose in the streets of St. Stephens, and Echo's legs were still shaking so badly she could hardly stand.

Wesley Vanderhoven was long gone. He merely walked down the steps, climbed into his car and drove away, leaving the chaos behind. But as soon as he left, the swirling emotion started to dissipate. The confusion. The helplessness. The insanity drained from her and Rand and the rest of the people on the street like water down a slow drain.

The last ambulance pulled away from the curb, taking one of the injured victims of road rage to the hospital. Rand finished his conversation with the St. Stephens officer who'd tried to come to their aid, and started making his way back to her.

The tremble spread up her legs and centered in her chest.

"How are you holding up?"

"Okay," she lied. "You?"

"Relieved, I guess. That I'm not losing my mind. The others were swept away with emotion as much as I was."

"That was what you were talking about. The emotional surge."

"Yes."

"Was Vanderhoven responsible all along?"

He shook his head. "I don't know. Maybe."

"Then that would mean…" Her stomach clutched. "Do you think he has Zoe? Do you think he's the one who kidnapped her?"

"I put an APB out for him. All law enforcement agencies in the area will be looking for him."

"But what good will that do? If he can amplify the cops' emotions to the point where they can't fight back, all the police on the Eastern Seaboard could be after him and it won't matter."

He rubbed his chin, fingertips scraping stubble. His eyes were sunken, the shadows around them dark as bruises. "I have to figure out a way to take him down. A way to get that weapon away from him."

"It's a weapon?" Of course. It made sense. If someone had a weapon like that, they could reduce an opposing army to a bunch of sobbing babies. "Is that what they were working on at Cranesbrook? I know they do research for the government. Are they developing weapons?"

Rand let out a breath. "It looks like Project Cypress is a weapon, yes. It's part of a contract Cranesbrook has with the DOD."

"How does it work?"

"I don't know. I don't know anything more than what I told you."

"But you're going to find out?"

"Yes."

"How? You said you aren't allowed inside Cranesbrook, right?"

"The St. Stephens PD has an officer watching the gate to the Cranesbrook campus. As soon as someone who can answer my questions leaves, they'll give my supervisor a call. That's how I found out Vanderhoven was on his way to see you."

A great plan. "I want to go with you. When you get the next call, I want to be there."

"You can't, Echo."

"Why not? If Vanderhoven has this weapon, if he is the one who kidnapped Zoe, don't you think I have the right to know what I'm up against?"

"You're a civilian. This is police business."

"I'm a mother and that monster has my child."

"No. I'm not going to let you endanger yourself."

"What about Zoe? What about the danger she's in?"

"No."

"You can't just expect me to sit around and do nothing."

"That's what you're going to have to do. I don't even know if *I* can convince anyone from Cranesbrook to give me straight answers. I know they aren't going to talk if you're there."

That might be true. But it felt like more than that. If felt like Rand was determined to keep her away from the people responsible. Determined to shut her out, as if keeping her helpless was for her own good. "Whatever we find out, I can handle it. What I can't handle is being kept in the dark."

"It's for the best."

"Who's best? Yours?"

"Echo…"

She held up her hands. "I know. I know. It's safer. You're protecting me."

"I *am* protecting you. I don't want to see you hurt."

"And having my baby out there, somewhere I can't reach her, that doesn't hurt? That doesn't kill me with every hour she's gone?"

He looked down at the ground. Creases lined his brow. Worry pinched the corners of his mouth. "I haven't known you long. I realize that. But the thought of you hurt, the thought of you gone…I can't live with that." He shook his head.

"Then you understand a little of how I feel about Zoe. About Bray."

"It's hell. I know. Believe me."

She did believe him. She could hear the ache of truth in his voice. But that much pain didn't come from his fear of losing her. It was deeper than that. Older. She remembered the story in the paper, the story she'd read before she'd met Detective Rand McClellan. "You're talking about your partner's death?"

"Richard Francis." He stared blankly at the cobblestone. For a long time he said nothing more. Finally, he raised his eyes to meet Echo's. "And Maxie Wallace."

"The other officer who was killed?"

"Yes. And there might be a third. An officer who was at Cranesbrook when Maxie died. He was found crying in the hall outside. He killed himself."

She gasped. She hadn't heard of the suicide. But after all that had happened, she knew what Rand was thinking. "Vanderhoven?"

He nodded.

She could understand his pain. Losing anyone was hard, people you worked with, people you liked. But there was more than loss in Rand's voice, in his expression. There was guilt. "And you believe if you had done something differently, they wouldn't be dead?"

"Maybe with Maxie. If I hadn't pushed for her help." He shook his head. "She was good police. I thought I was doing her a favor."

"You can't blame yourself for that."

"I know. It doesn't make a lot of sense." He shook his head again, as if trying to discount all he'd revealed.

"There's more to it than that, isn't there?"

"I don't want to talk about this, Echo."

"Why not? Maybe you need to talk. Maybe you need to get these feelings out instead of keeping them bottled up."

"No, I need to focus on this case. Find the bastards responsible. And keep you safe."

"By keeping me sitting at home when I could be doing something to find my little girl."

"You're going to have to trust me, Echo." He blew a stream of air through tight lips. "It's the only way."

RAND HAD JUST DROPPED Echo off at her house when the call came through. Nelson Ulrich had driven out of the front gate at Cranesbrook and was heading toward his residence along the water not far from downtown St. Stephens.

Pushing his troubling discussion with Echo to the back of his mind, Rand caught up to Cranesbrook's director of research in front of his condo on the St. Stephens Harbor. The afternoon sun gleamed off his bare scalp and the graying blond hair combed over to conceal it. The scent of crab cakes wafted from the restaurant take-out container in his hand, reminding Rand of just how long it had been since he'd taken time to eat.

"Nelson Ulrich? I'm with the state police. I need to ask you a few questions."

Ulrich didn't slow his pace. His white lab coat flapped in the light breeze, the buttons skewed as if he'd fastened them in a hurry. "I would like to eat my dinner, if you don't mind…detective, is it?"

Rand fell into step beside him. "Detective McClellan."

"Ah, yes. The man who shot Sid." He didn't wait for an answer. "I trust you received the surveillance video from Hank Riddell."

"Yes."

"And that you'll find Mr. Sloane."

"We're working on it."

"Good. Maybe you will get the opportunity to use some of your expert marksmanship on him."

"At least I don't have to ask how you feel about Bray Sloane."

"Feel? How should I feel? The man tried to sabotage one of my laboratories."

"Allegedly." He almost wished Echo was here so she could appreciate his restraint.

Ulrich stopped at the entrance to the condo's lobby and grasped the door handle. "Detective, I know what I saw on that DVD. I would hope that as a police officer,

you, too, know evidence when you see it."
Ulrich peered through his wire-rimmed
glasses as if looking down on a servant.

A good trick since Rand was at least an
inch or two taller. "The video is damning.
I agree." Add that to Sloane's debt situation
and it added up to likely guilt, whether
Echo wanted to acknowledge it or not.

"Then I trust that justice will be served."
He bobbed his head in a sharp nod, as if everything was settled.

Rand didn't move.

Ulrich gave him an impatient glower.
"Is there anything else?"

"I heard that Wesley Vanderhoven
visited you this morning."

Ulrich didn't answer for so long, Rand
thought he might not have heard his statement. "Did he visit you?"

"Yes, he did."

"Why?" Judging from how uncomfortable talk of Vanderhoven made Ulrich,
Rand would be willing to bet the research
director knew something. Though what
that might be, he couldn't tell.

Ulrich stepped away from the door. Leading Rand around the side of the condo, he stopped at a small patio with a view of the water. White swans dotted the still blue. "I could make up some nice story, but you'd see through that, wouldn't you, Detective?"

"I'd like to think so."

"And I can trust you not to mention this information to anyone? Our investors would be rather upset." His thin lips stretched into a phony smile.

"I don't run in the same social circles as your investors, Ulrich. You have nothing to worry about."

"Very well." He paused as if searching for the right words. "Vanderhoven threatened me."

The lab tech was full of surprises today. "Threatened you? How?"

"With a lawsuit. As a result of the explosion. I don't have to tell you that something like that could cost the company a great deal, both in dollars and in reputation."

So Vanderhoven hadn't used the emotional amplification weapon against Ulrich? Or was that part of the threat? A part Ulrich didn't want to mention. "So you're going to pay him off?"

Ulrich brushed his question away the way he might shoo a pesky fly. "Kelso deals with that end."

"Dr. Martin Kelso."

"He wanted Edmonston's title, he gets Edmonston's problems."

"And you? You didn't want the title?" As dedicated to research as Ulrich seemed, he also seemed to have a healthy desire for power. Just the way he looked down at Rand suggested that much.

"Research, Detective. That's what's important to me. Science. I didn't get this far to become a paper pusher."

"Then maybe you can tell me something."

He raised a graying blond brow.

"Strange things have been happening lately. I wonder if you can help shed some light on them. From a scientific perspective."

"I'll certainly try."

"Could there be a chemical agent of some kind that could alter people's emotions?"

Ulrich didn't even blink. "Of course. Have you heard of alcohol? Not to mention certain prescription drugs and a whole host of illegal ones."

"I'm not talking about drugs. Well, none that I'm familiar with. This would be some kind of airborne agent."

Ulrich stopped and looked at him as if for the first time. "Maybe if you give me some particulars…"

"I first noticed the effect in the Beech Grove Clinic."

"And what was the effect exactly? How were your emotions altered?"

Rand hesitated. He was here to ask Ulrich the questions, not vice versa. But he needed to know what he was dealing with. And if anyone could tell him, it was Cranesbrook's director of research. Whether he *would* tell was something else. "They weren't altered as much as exaggerated. As if any small thing I felt was amplified."

"How strong was this amplification?"

"Strong enough that it was very hard to control."

"Or impossible?"

His gut seized at the memory. The sensation of being so overwhelmed by feeling that nothing else mattered. The last time, just hours ago in the street outside Echo's shop, he'd been so out of his mind he hadn't even been able to get his body to work. "Yes. Impossible."

"Interesting."

"I believe it might be a drug administered through the air. Possibly something being tested at Beech Grove. Or Cranesbrook."

Ulrich's brows arched toward his comb over. "I would be very surprised if Dr. Frederick Morton had such creativity."

So he knew Morton, too. Or at least knew of him. "How about Wesley Vanderhoven?"

"Maybe. He's a brilliant young man, if a bit…immature."

"So it is something Vanderhoven was working on at Cranesbrook?"

He shook his head. "I assure you, we

don't have such a thing in development. And I would know."

"Not that you would tell me if you did."

"No, probably not." The corner of his mouth twitched. "But I'm curious."

"About what?"

"If we were developing such a drug, as you say, what would be the purpose? It seems that there's enough emotion in the world. Why would we want to amplify it?"

Rand thought of the scene outside Maritime Lullaby. It hadn't just been him and Echo. The St. Stephens cop hadn't been able to draw his gun. The victims of the car crash had beaten the pulp out of one another. "Extreme emotion can debilitate."

"So you're thinking this amplification could be used as a weapon?"

"That's what you do at Cranesbrook, isn't it? Create chemical weapons for the government?"

"We do a great many things."

"For the Department of Defense."

He nodded his head to the side, conceding the issue. "They are a client."

"Is that what Project Cypress is? A way to use the enemy's emotions to bring them to their knees?"

Ulrich chuckled and shook his head. "I'm afraid you've been reading far too much science fiction, Detective. The DOD would never weaponize emotions. Emotions are far too unpredictable."

Rand couldn't disagree there. "So what is this chemical agent, Dr. Ulrich? And why does your lab technician have it?"

"Wesley Vanderhoven?"

"Yes."

"I'm afraid I don't know of a chemical agent that can amplify emotions in others. Sorry. And as for Wesley Vanderhoven, I can't say I understand where he's coming from anymore. I wish I did."

ECHO CURLED ON HER COUCH, clutching Zoe's stuffed bear to her chest. She looked at the officer drinking coffee and nibbling cookies and cakes neighbors had dropped off to help with her ordeal.

Rand had made sure she had someone

with her. She couldn't even take control of protecting herself and monitoring the phone. She'd never felt so helpless. And considering her life lately, that was saying a lot.

A knock sounded on the door. A rap so light she almost missed it.

The officer pushed back from the table.

"I can get it." Probably a neighbor with more carbohydrates. She thrust herself up from the couch and crossed to the front window. Pulling the front drapery aside, she peeked out into the waning afternoon light.

A young woman with short blond hair stood on the front step. Dressed in jeans and a poncho, she rubbed her arms as if she was cold. Or nervous.

The officer pulled open the door.

Echo stepped up beside him. "Hello?"

The woman nodded to the officer and turned nervous eyes on Echo. "Ms. Sloane? I was wondering if I could talk to you."

The woman looked very familiar, but for the life of her, Echo couldn't place where she'd seen her. "I'm sorry, I don't remember your name."

Again, she looked at the officer, as if she might want to bolt instead of admitting her name to the police. "I sort of met you at the Beech Grove Clinic."

Her face registered in Echo's mind, along with a whiff of lemon in the air. It was the disheveled blonde they'd met coming out of Wes Vanderhoven's room. She didn't look so disheveled now. Now she looked worried. And obviously shaken by the officer's presence.

"Yes, I remember. It's nice of you to drop by." Echo glanced at the officer then back to the woman. "You know, I'm hungry for crab cakes and French fries. There's this great seafood place just two blocks down that is supposed to have wonderful greasy food. Do you want to walk down there with me?"

The woman nodded her cropped blond head. "Sure."

Echo glanced up at the officer. The thought of eating made her sick to her stomach. But she feigned what she hoped was a hungry look. "Can I get you something? You can't live on cakes and cookies alone."

He laid a hand on his fit belly. "No, thanks. I've eaten enough for a week. But take your cell phone. I might need to get in touch."

The phone. She let out a breath. She was glad Rand hadn't given the cop instructions to keep her in sight at all times. Of course, what would be the point? If Vanderhoven wanted to reach her, he could do so anytime he wanted—even if her house was full of cops.

Tucking her cell into her purse, Echo and the woman started to walk the two blocks to Sam's Crab Shack. "What is your name?" Echo asked.

"Ashley Kromm."

"What did you want to talk to me about, Ashley?"

"I was fired from Beech Grove today."

"Fired? Why?"

"Nurse Dumont wouldn't say. But I think it's because I saw stuff I wasn't supposed to. My grandmother urged me to tell someone."

"What did you see?"

"I heard the detective you were with asking Dr. Morton about Mr. Darnell. About them keeping his arms and legs tied."

"Yes?"

"I cared for him several times. He was tied. Even when he was asleep."

"Was he violent, like the doctor said?"

She shook her head. "He was when they brought him in. Wesley was, too. But even after they quieted down, they were tied."

Rand would want to hear that. Maybe Ashley's testimony to that would be enough to charge the doctor for something. "Will you tell the detective about this?"

"I don't know…"

"Doctor Morton and Nurse Dumont have to be stopped, Ashley. They have to be held accountable for what they've done. You could make sure they are."

"I…I really can't."

"Why not?"

"Because they fired me. They'll just say I'm trying to get back at them."

Echo narrowed her eyes. Ashley must

not be telling her everything. Otherwise, the young nurse's logic didn't make much sense. "But they fired you for seeing their illegal activities. You're obligated to blow the whistle."

They stopped on a footbridge over a stream. Ashley shifted her weight from one foot to the other, as if she was reconsidering their whole discussion.

Echo grew more uneasy with each second that passed. "That *is* why they fired you, right?"

"Well, not entirely."

"What haven't you told me?"

Ashley's cheeks flushed with pink.

Echo touched Ashley's arm. "It's okay. I won't tell anyone if you don't want me to."

Ashley leaned against the railing and shifted her feet. "It was Nurse Dumont. She caught me doing something I shouldn't have done."

"What?"

"I made love with a patient." She held up her hands in an attempt to head off Echo's judgments. "But it wasn't something lewd and disgusting, like Dumont said. And it wasn't a one-time fling, either. He needs me. We really care for each other. He's so smart. And he thinks I'm beautiful."

Echo gripped the bridge's narrow steel rail. The cold numbed her hand and traveled up her arm. "The patient was Wesley Vanderhoven, wasn't it? That's why you looked so disheveled the day I saw you at Beech Grove. You were… making love before we got there."

Dipping her chin, Ashley stared at the water rushing in the stream below.

It all made sense. Far too much sense, if you asked Echo. "So he used it on you."

"Used what?"

Echo studied Ashley's pink-stained cheeks. The poor woman was infatuated with Vanderhoven. She thought the uncontrollable feelings he inspired in her were real attraction. Even love. In reality, Vanderhoven had just started the spark with a soft-porn movie and fanned the flames from there.

Echo could hardly tell Ashley her

feelings weren't real. Especially since she had no idea what *was* real, exactly. Or how to describe what Vanderhoven was doing.

"Used what?" Ashley repeated.

Echo shook her head. "Nothing. Where is Wesley now?"

"I don't know. I haven't seen him since this morning when he borrowed my car."

How convenient for Vanderhoven. A cute blond nurse who would provide sex *and* a vehicle. Echo set her purse on the railing and dug inside for a card. "If you see him, I want you to call me. Right away. Okay?" She located a card and handed it to Ashley.

Ashley looked at it as if Echo offered a poisoned apple. "Why? Is he in trouble?"

"He might have stolen a very dangerous chemical. A chemical he's used to commit crimes."

"Crimes?" Ashley wrinkled her nose. "Wesley wouldn't commit crimes."

Echo took a deep breath. Now she knew how Rand felt trying to convince her that Bray was guilty of wrongdoing. The only difference was that Wes Vanderhoven actually *was* guilty. "I believe Wesley kidnapped my baby."

"No."

Echo nodded. "I was there. He had his face covered by a dark ski mask, but I'm pretty sure it was Wesley."

"You're lying!" Ashley swiped at the card, knocking it from Echo's grip. Her hand hit Echo's purse, sending it over the railing.

Echo watched her black vinyl bag splash into the water below.

"I don't believe you. I'll never believe you." Ashley turned and raced over the bridge and turned down a side street.

Echo started after her. "Ashley, wait!"

But Ashley was already gone.

Chapter Twelve

"Where is she?" Rand focused on the St. Stephens officer sitting alone in Echo's kitchen. He'd been worried about Echo all evening, wanting to race back to her house to make sure she was all right. Yet at the same time, he wanted to stay away. After their run-in with Vanderhoven, he'd revealed more than he should have. He couldn't help it. He was beginning to think that where Echo was concerned, his usual defenses and cool logic were useless.

But after his meeting with Ulrich and tying up other business with the investigation that he absolutely had to attend to, his worry for her had won out. It had never occurred to him, now that he was finally here, that she would be gone.

"She went to get something to eat," the officer answered.

Rand eyed Echo's kitchen. Cakes and cookies and every kind of pie he could imagine heaped the countertops. And he happened to know the refrigerator was equally filled with casseroles. The whole neighborhood had poured out its support for Echo in the form of food. If she wanted something to eat, the last place she needed to go was out.

Of course, knowing Echo the way he was starting to, he could imagine her going on an errand just to keep herself feeling occupied and useful. But that didn't mean the cop should have allowed it. "You let her go out alone?"

"A friend stopped by. They two of them went together."

"A friend? What was the name?"

"Didn't ask."

"You let her go out with just anyone?"

The cop gave him a incredulous look.

"I'm not her father, and she's not in protective custody. I didn't know I should have tied her down."

Rand shook his head. He was getting out of hand. He was caring too much. Worrying too much. After what had happened this afternoon, he could hardly see straight. "Sorry."

The cop held up a hand, warding off more apologies. "The friend was a woman. Youngish. Short blond hair. She said something about having met Echo at Beech Grove, whatever that is."

Beech Grove? The young nurse? The one who had smelled like lemon?

Leave it to Echo to turn a simple run for food into an investigation. And seeing that the nurse worked for Dr. Morton, it could prove to be a dangerous investigation.

The beat of his pulse rose in his ears. "Does Echo have her cell?"

"Yeah."

Rand pulled out his own cell phone and punched in her number, a number he knew by heart though he'd never called it. The phone on the other end rang and rang. No answer. No voice mail.

Adrenaline spiked his blood like a shot of espresso. He was about to try again when Echo's home phone rang.

Rand lunged to pick up the receiver and brought it to his ear. He wanted to shout Echo's name, demand to know where she was, that she was okay. Instead he took a deep breath. "Sloane residence."

A click sounded and the line went dead. Damn.

Behind him, the front door opened. Echo stepped inside.

Rand spun around. "Where the hell have you been?" He crossed the room in four strides.

Echo searched his face, her eyes widening with alarm. "What happened?"

"You missed a phone call."

"The kidnapper?"

"No, I don't think so." Rand glanced up at the cop in the kitchen and willed his heart rate to slow. "Got a number?"

The cop leaned down to read the display

on Echo's Caller ID. "Got it. Not the same number. It's a cell phone, though." He read off the digits.

Rand had seen that number recently. And he had a hunch where. He pulled out his notebook and found the card he'd taken at Cranesbrook. "That's Claire Fanshaw's cell."

"Claire Fanshaw?" Echo repeated. "That's the woman Bray argued with. The woman from Cranesbrook."

"And we can only hope she has some information." Rand pulled out his phone and punched in the number, glad to have something to focus on that didn't concern Echo directly. Or his worry for her. The phone rang, finally ending with a voice-mail message. He disconnected without leaving a word.

"Aren't you going to ask why she called?"

He'd considered it, but if Claire didn't pick up after just having called, it probably meant her fleeting moment of trust and cooperation was gone. "I'll talk to her tomorrow morning. Claire has a talent for lying. It's always better to deal with someone like that in person rather than on the phone."

"No wonder Bray didn't like her. Ever since our dad, he's hated people who lie."

Rand didn't think he'd bring up the way Brayden had lied to Echo about the state of his finances. The last thing he needed was to get into another no-win argument with her over her brother. "Why didn't you answer your phone?"

"Oh." She raised her purse in front of him. "Ashley Kromm knocked it into the stream a couple of blocks down. My phone drowned."

"Ashley Kromm is the nurse? The one we saw leaving Vanderhoven's room?"

She nodded and filled him in on the story of Ashley Kromm. "She wouldn't listen to me. She might know where Vanderhoven is right now. She might be in danger. But she wouldn't tell me a thing. She just ran." She lowered herself to the couch. Pulling her legs up under her, she pulled Zoe's stuffed toy onto her lap.

Rand fought the urge to sit beside her.

"McClellan? Hate to interrupt, but my shift is over."

Rand nodded to the officer. "I'll take over. Go ahead."

As soon as the cop left, Rand turned back to Echo. She looked small and vulnerable, curled on the couch holding that stuffed seahorse that had to have come from Maritime Lullaby. He ached to wrap her in his arms. Exactly what he couldn't do. "You're still worrying about Ashley Kromm, aren't you?"

"Vanderhoven can do anything he wants to her. He probably doesn't even have to use his emotion amplification drug. She thinks she's in love with him. She won't believe anything I said."

He nodded.

"I know what you're thinking."

He doubted it. *He* didn't even know what he was thinking half the time. Not anymore. "What am I thinking?"

"That I have the same kind of blind allegiance to my brother."

He might have thought that. If he'd had some distance. If he could rip his focus from the way she curled her legs under her on the couch, the way she held on to that seahorse, the openness and vulnerability that radiated from her. "I know you love your brother, Echo. I know how much he means to you. I would never belittle that."

"So how do you deal with all of this?"

He perched on the edge of the coffee table in front of her, close enough to look into her eyes, yet far enough to keep the temptation of touching her on the far edge of his mind. "Deal with what?"

"Knowing all these horrible things might be happening and being helpless to control them?"

"I focus on what I can do."

"And the rest doesn't bother you?"

"Of course it does." More than she could know. "But dwelling on it isn't going to help."

She let out a heavy breath. "I hate it. Being helpless. It makes me feel like I did as a kid."

From what she'd let slip before, he could

guess the time in her childhood she was referring to. "When your dad left."

She pressed her lips together in a sad smile.

He couldn't imagine any man leaving Echo. Not her father, and not the father of her baby. She was so open and honest and beautiful. He couldn't imagine how anyone could look into those tender gray eyes and then turn around and deliberately cause her pain.

He, on the other hand, was coming from a very different place. A very different background. "In my family, things would have been better if my father *had* left."

She lowered her brows and searched his face. "What did he do?"

He didn't realize he'd mentioned his father out loud until she spoke. He waved her question away. "That was a stupid thing to say. Forget it."

"Not stupid. You can tell me."

He'd never talked about it. Not with the cops who'd come to the door that night. Not with the handful of shrinks he'd been forced to see afterward. Not even with his mother. He'd hated the sympathetic looks. The pity. The compassion he didn't begin to deserve. But something inside him wanted to tell Echo.

All the more reason he shouldn't. "Really, it's nothing. I just didn't get along with my old man."

"Did he hit you?"

"Hit me? No. He was a good guy. A good cop."

"The reason you went into law enforcement?"

"Yeah."

She reached for his hand and brushed her fingers gently over his wrist. Looking up into his face, she searched his eyes, her mouth pinching with concern. "Then why do you wish he'd left?"

He shook his head. He was an idiot for saying anything. It had just seemed so natural to talk to Echo, to blurt out what he was feeling. Echo made him feel so much he couldn't keep things wrapped inside. "I really shouldn't have brought it up."

"Was he killed?"

He let out a breath. "He died when I was a kid."

"So you lost your dad, too."

"Not in the way you did. You didn't deserve to have your father walk out like that. You didn't deserve to have him make you feel that way."

She looked down at their hands. Fitting her fingers between his, she twined her hand with his. "I wasn't referring to my dad. I was talking about you losing Richard Francis and Maxie Wallace. You lost your father, too. Another cop."

He'd never related Richard's and Maxie's and Officer Woodard's deaths to that of his father.

"Do you feel responsible for your father's death, too?"

Her question sliced into him like a well-honed blade. He wanted to say no. He wanted to push her away. He wanted to shove the whole mess out of his mind and never think of it again.

Instead he just sat there like an idiot and said nothing.

She leaned toward him, her skin soft on his. Warm. Accepting. "Why? You were a kid when your father died, right? How old were you?"

"Thirteen." His voice sounded rough, hoarse with emotion. Emotion he didn't want to feel.

"So how could you possibly be responsible?"

She made him want to let his guard down, want to tell her things no one should know. Things he couldn't even accept himself.

"Was he killed on the job?"

"He was on disability."

"Disability?" Her eyebrows dipped over those clear, gray eyes. "How did he die?"

He hesitated. How in the world had he ever thought he could explain this? He didn't want to think about his father. Didn't want to get lost in the flood of emotions that came with the memories.

The flood of guilt and regret that would sweep him away.

"You can tell me, Rand. Sometimes it helps just saying things out loud."

It wouldn't help. He knew it wouldn't. It would only bring his guilt front and center. It would only show Echo the man he really was. It would only push her away. "He committed suicide, Echo. My father killed himself."

Her fingers tightened around his. "I'm so sorry, Rand."

He shook his head. "Don't feel sorry. Not for me."

"Why not?"

"Because I don't deserve it."

"What do you mean?"

He didn't say anything. He couldn't force the words out. He didn't want to hear them.

"Rand?" She dipped her head and looked upward, trying to read his eyes. "Your father was an adult. He was responsible for his own actions."

"I wish it were that simple."

"It is."

He shook his head. "My dad suffered from severe depression. He spent most of his time either in psychiatrists' offices or in his bedroom. It got so bad he had to go on disability. He couldn't even work."

"It must have been horrible."

"I'm sure it was horrible…for him. I made it horrible."

"What are you saying?"

A bitter taste hung in his mouth. A flavor he'd been living with for the last twenty years. "I wanted a dad like other kids had. A dad who did things with me. A dad who took me to ball games and spoke at my school for career day. I wished he was the tough cop he used to be. Someone I could look up to."

"You were a kid. It's natural you felt that way."

"If wishing was as far as it went."

She didn't answer. All he could hear was her soft breathing, as if she was waiting for him to go on. Waiting for him to explain what he'd done.

He didn't want to go on. He didn't want to feel these things, let alone talk about them. But somehow he knew he no longer had that choice. "I told him how I felt. All of it. I told him I was ashamed he was my father."

Her grip didn't falter. She didn't turn away.

"That night he put his shotgun in his mouth and pulled the trigger." He could still see the scene when he and his mother had rushed into the bedroom. He could still smell the gunpowder and the warm scent of blood. "So you see, it would have been better if he'd just walked away. Better for me and far, far better for him."

The clock in the corner ticked away the time. One minute. Two. Finally Echo leaned back in the couch, pulling at his hand. "Will you sit with me? Hold me?"

He looked at her, trying to read her eyes, trying to figure out what was going on in that beautiful head. He'd expected her to react, but not like this. "Did you hear what I said?"

"Yes."

"I caused my father's death. I caused him to take his own life."

The corners of her lips tilted up in a smile full of sadness. "I think it's ironic how my father left me feeling helpless and yours left you feeling you had more power than any kid could ever have."

He opened his mouth to disagree, to make her understand, to…what? He wasn't sure. He closed it without saying a word.

She pulled his hand. "Just sit with me. Hold me. Maybe between the two of us, we'll end up neither helpless nor responsible for everything. Maybe between the two of us, we'll end up just right."

Chapter Thirteen

Rand awoke the next morning on the couch next to Echo, still cradling her in his arms. And although he didn't remember a time when he'd ever stayed all night with a woman without making love to her, he had to admit the night with Echo had felt just right.

As if, for at least one moment in time, he'd tasted peace.

Of course, in the light of day, reality rushed back. And as he'd done since he was thirteen, he dealt with it the only way he knew. He pushed it to the back of his mind. "I need to talk to Claire Fanshaw, find out what she called about last night."

Echo rubbed her eyes and padded to the

kitchen on stocking feet. After dumping coffee beans into the grinder, she turned it on. "When are you going?"

He picked up his navy jacket from the back of the chair where he'd draped it. "As soon as I have a cup of coffee."

She nodded and poured water into the coffeemaker.

He should duck out without the coffee. Alone. But somehow it didn't feel right. After last night, he couldn't leave Echo helplessly waiting for him to bring her baby home. Not when he was sure she wanted to help. Needed to help.

Besides, he couldn't handle the thought of her here by herself. Unprotected. "Do you want to come? I could use your help."

A smile curved her lips and crinkled the corners of those sparkling eyes. "I'll get ready."

It didn't take long for Echo to change into a fresh pair of jeans and another one of those light, gauzy tops that made Rand want to touch her. Soon the two of them were climbing from his sedan and scanning the Breezy Cove Marina, a small docking facility nestled on an inlet on Chesapeake Bay. Moving his gaze over the white, red-roofed building that held a café, supply store, bath house and laundry, and past the playground and covered pavilion, Rand focused on the first of seven docks stretching into the water.

Echo emerged from the car and slammed the passenger door. "Claire Fanshaw lives on a boat?"

It was all Rand could do to keep from focusing on Echo. Instead, he trained his gaze on the docks. "This is the address I have for her. The boat is called *Lainie's Moor.*" Rand spotted the thirty-four-foot Sea Ray Sundancer in a slip on the dock closest to the parking lot. He extended a finger, pointing out the small craft. "There it is."

The two of them started for the dock. Halfway there, Echo slowed her steps.

"What's wrong?"

"I was just thinking. She called *me* last night, not you. Maybe she knows something she doesn't want to share with the police. Maybe I should talk to her alone."

"Alone? Not a chance." The whole reason he'd brought her along was to protect her. Even thinking about those moments before Echo had returned home last night—how worried he was, how out of his mind with fear—made him cringe. He wasn't about to let her out of his sight again. Not unless he knew she'd be safer without him. "We'll convince her to talk. I've won her trust before. At least a sliver of it. Between the two of us, we'll win it again."

"But what if she can't tell you?"

"You mean, what if she has information about something illegal?" She didn't have to answer. He knew that was what she meant. "Then she'll be doing herself a favor in the long run by talking to me now."

She shifted her gaze to the water.

"Does this mean you're willing to consider that Bray could be involved in something shady?" he asked.

"No. I'll never believe that."

Rand would give almost anything for

Bray Sloane to be the great guy his sister thought he was. Just the thought of Echo's heartbreak if her brother turned out to be guilty made Rand want to do anything in his power to shield her. But with the evidence stacking up against Bray Sloane, Rand realized he might not be able to protect Echo from that sorrow. "Echo, we'll find your brother, and we'll get Zoe back. Then we'll figure out what to do from there. Deal?"

She drew in a shaky breath. Pressing her lips into a tight smile, she nodded. "Bray will do whatever is in his power to help. I know he will. And I also know that whatever happened at Cranesbrook wasn't his fault." Her voice ached with love, with worry.

Worry not unlike what Rand had felt last night for Echo. "Let's find out what Claire Fanshaw has to say." He turned into the cool breeze blowing off the Chesapeake and walked the rest of the way to the slip holding *Lainie's Moor.* Echo matched him stride for stride, their footfalls reverberating on the wood planks. The redhead emerged on deck before they reached the boat.

"Excuse me, Ms. Fanshaw."

"Can I—" She focused on Rand. Her eyes flew wide. "Detective McClellan."

"Echo and I stopped by to see what you called about last night."

She glanced at Echo and then back to Rand. She bit her lower lip for a moment, then smoothed her mouth into a practiced smile. "I just wanted to know how the investigation was going."

"Why not call *my* cell phone, then? You called Echo."

"I mislaid your card. But I knew with Echo's baby missing, she'd probably be able to get in touch with you for me." The smile dropped from her lips and she focused on Echo. "Besides, I wanted to tell you how sorry I am to hear what you're going through."

"Thanks."

Claire's sympathy for Echo's plight seemed genuine, heightening his sense that everything that had come before was not.

"It still seems strange to me that you would call Echo for an update on the case. Especially since the two of you haven't met."

She looked over her shoulder, down the steps leading to the boat's cabin. "That's what telephone directories are for."

He still wasn't buying it. And her apparent nervousness wasn't helping convince him. "I think you found out something. Something you're not eager to share with the police."

She glanced down at her watch. "Um, I'm going to be late for work."

"You're going to be even later if you have to make a stop at the state police barracks."

"All I did was make a phone call."

"And hang up when I answered."

"I didn't know it was you. I didn't know who it was."

Because she hadn't give him an opportunity to tell her. "If you were trying to reach me through Echo, why would hearing my voice surprise you?"

"I thought I would just talk to her, tell her how sorry I was and everything. Besides, I've been tense."

"About what?"

Claire looked around again. "If you don't mind, I don't really want all my neighbors to know my business."

Echo stepped up next to Rand. Reaching out, she laid a hand on Claire's forearm. "If you know something, anything, please…"

"I really have to get to work." Claire glanced back at the boat. "Walk with me to my car." Without waiting for his assent, she started in the direction of the parking lot. Rand and Echo fell in, one on either side.

Claire didn't speak until they had cleared the dock and were crossing the blacktop. Even then, her voice was hushed. "I don't have any proof."

"Of what?" Rand prodded.

"I saw a money transfer. It was put through the day of the accident in Lab 7."

"A money transfer? From Cranesbrook?"

She nodded. "To Dr. Frederick Morton at the Beech Grove Clinic. Isn't that the mental hospital where that murder happened?"

It sure was. "What was the dollar amount on the transfer?"

"Two mil."

"Two million dollars?" Echo responded.

Claire shrugged a shoulder. "Cranesbrook deals in large transactions all the time, but most of them aren't to medical facilities. I'm not sure why it went to a doctor rather than to the clinic itself."

Rand was pretty sure. "So why didn't you mention this earlier?"

"Just because a transfer that large isn't common doesn't mean it's not on the up-and-up. Besides, I shouldn't be sharing Cranesbrook financial records."

Echo asked the obvious question. "So why are you sharing this information now?"

Claire paused, as if waiting to deliver the punch line. "Because it disappeared."

"The record of the transfer disappeared?" Rand's pulse accelerated, thrumming in his ears. "When?"

"Yesterday. Normally I wouldn't have thought much of it since I work in computers, not accounting. But with that murder at the clinic, the whole thing struck me as strange."

Strange? He'd say. It was also the piece of evidence he needed to nail Dr. Morton. And if he was lucky, the answer to who else at Cranesbrook might want to cover up the truth behind Project Cypress.

Echo peered at Rand, hope beaming from those soft gray eyes. "They say you can't fully erase files off a hard drive."

Claire nodded. "You can't."

"Can you get a warrant for those computers? Prove they paid big bucks to the clinic to hold those men against their will?" Echo was dreaming, and she looked like she knew it.

Rand only wished he could tell her she was wrong, that warrants were possible. "I'm afraid Cranesbrook is off limits."

Echo let out a long breath.

"Off-limits?" Claire parroted. "Who told you that?"

"The feds. As a detective with the state police, I'm afraid my hands are tied." But just because the evidence no longer existed, that didn't mean the revelation was useless. Not when he combined it with skills he'd picked up at the poker table.

Morton's high-stakes games were about to end.

RAND EXPLAINED his idea to Echo on the drive to Beech Grove.

"Do you really think you can get him to admit to holding Gage Darnell against his will?"

"If I make it seem a confession is in his best interest." He shrugged a shoulder, trying to convince himself as much as Echo that this would be easy. Or at least doable. "He doesn't have to know I can't access records of the money transfer. If we're lucky, the fact that I know about it will be damning enough."

"What about Beech Grove's records? Is there a record of the transfer there?"

"We've been through the Beech Grove records. Besides the money was transferred directly to Morton."

"Can you search his bank records?"

"Not without probable cause."

"And Claire's word isn't?"

"Not when it can't be corroborated."

"Like with a confession?" Echo smiled, her face beaming with hope, despite all she'd faced in the past days.

Rand's chest tightened. He was getting in way over his head. He'd figured that out this morning when he woke with Echo in his arms. But he had to keep swimming. No matter what happened, he couldn't let Echo down. "I like the way you think. Let's get a confession."

When they reached the clinic, they found Morton in a patient's room.

"I need a word with you, doctor," Rand said.

The short man shot him an annoyed look, but followed him into the hall, out of his patient's earshot. "Why are you here this time, detective? You can expect a harassment suit if this doesn't end right now."

"I'm here to end it, Morton. Though probably not in the way you hope."

The doctor's eyes shifted. He dug his

hand into a pocket, pulling out his ever-present mints. Judging from the way his hand shook when he popped the candy in his mouth, the good doctor wasn't as good at bluffing as he might like to think.

Rand couldn't help but smile. He loved playing poker. And he loved taking down bad guys. Especially ones that were smug and rich. "You might want to do this behind closed doors. Somewhere you can sit down."

Morton led them back to the entrance and strode into his office ahead of them. Once inside, he remained on his feet next to the desk, a man making his last stand.

Fine with Rand. He peered out the open window at the police cruiser pulling up to the door. Just in time.

Echo glanced up at him. She'd seen the backup, too.

"What's going on in here?" Nurse Dumont's voice rang through the length of the hall. She bullied her way into the office before Rand got the chance to close the door.

Rand nodded to the nurse. "I'm glad you're here. Why don't you join us?"

On the other side of the office, Morton glared a silent message to his nurse.

Rand looked from Morton to Dumont and back again. "I know Cranesbrook Associates wired you two million dollars after the lab accident."

"That was for patient care," Doctor Morton said.

"It went to you. Not Beech Grove. The clinic's own records show you also contacted Darnell's and Vanderhoven's insurance companies. That's double dipping, Doctor. And a very healthy double dip at that."

Nurse Dumont blew a stream of air through her nose. She glared at the doctor.

"It was an administrative mix-up. Nothing more." He popped another mint.

"In addition, Echo had an interesting discussion with Ashley Kromm."

Nurse Dumont folded thick arms across her chest. "Ashley was fired for inappropriate and unprofessional behavior. She obviously would say anything to strike back at the clinic."

"Perhaps. But it's exactly what she said

that's interesting to me. It seems she corroborates Gage Darnell's story."

Dumont shook her head so hard, she nearly lost her glasses. "She never took care of Darnell."

"Or Vanderhoven?"

Dumont lowered her chin.

"According to Ms. Kromm, both patients were tied down. Even when they were sleeping."

Morton scoffed. "You saw Vanderhoven. Did he look tied down to you? Did he look like he was being kept prisoner?"

"No. Not by the time I saw him. But I'll get to him in a minute." Rand paused for what he hoped was dramatic effect. "Ms. Kromm also admits to feeling unnaturally strong emotions. The possible effects of some kind of drug being tested on her."

"This again?" Morton slammed a fist on his desk. "I don't know anything about a drug that intensifies emotions. I never experimented on anyone. She's lying."

"Isn't it true that's what the money from Cranesbrook was for? They developed a chemical weapon that amplified people's emotions, and you tested it on your patients?"

"No, it isn't true." Morton's complexion deepened to a dark pink.

"Then how do you explain the two million dollars?"

"That wasn't for experimentation."

"What was it for?"

He sucked hard on his mints and said nothing.

"I have enough to shut down your clinic, Morton. It's not just Gage Darnell now. Now I have other witnesses. Money transfers. You're looking at time. But if someone else is involved, you can do yourself a favor with the state's attorney if you name names."

Morton stared at the floor, his scalp red through his thinning hair.

Rand shrugged a shoulder, portraying a nonchalance he didn't feel. "Up to you. I'd rather you didn't roll over, to tell you the truth. I can't tell you how disgusting I find people like you. People who get their kicks from rummaging around in a man's mind, stirring up his emotions, until he doesn't know up from down."

Echo put a hand on his arm.

He didn't need her reminder to realize he wasn't only talking about Morton anymore. But he appreciated her touch all the same. Her support. Her caring.

"I didn't test anything on anyone," Morton said. "You can talk to my lawyer. He'll explain it to you. I'm done wasting my breath."

The cold ache of failure sank into Rand's bones. Damn. He'd known he would run the risk of badgering Morton into lawyering up. He'd hoped the doctor would crack first. Now with a lawyer onboard, merely the threat of evidence would get Rand nowhere. Damn lawyers tended to insist on the evidence itself.

He glanced at Echo. He'd hit another dead end. If he couldn't get more information out of Morton, he was no closer to finding Zoe than he had been last night.

"I can answer your questions." Nurse

Dumont's sharp voice cut through the office. "But I want a deal from the state's attorney. A plea bargain."

Morton glared at her. "Shut up."

She looked at him as if his words meant as much to her as the buzzing of a bug. "No jail time. Not if you want me to say what I know in court."

Rand nodded, trying not to seem too eager, too desperate. "I'll recommend it."

The two St. Stephens officers stepped into the doorway.

Rand nodded to them and then to the nurse. "Go on."

She peered over her glasses at Morton. "He forced me to help him. If I didn't go along, he told me I'd lose my job."

"You lying bitch." Morton shifted his weight as if itching to run away. "I paid her. She made good money to keep that damn trap shut."

"I sure didn't make any two million dollars." She turned back to Rand. "Sid Edmonston paid him to keep them here. Make sure they wouldn't tell what happened."

"What *did* happen?" Echo prodded.

Dumont shook her head. "All I know is Edmonston didn't want anyone to know about the accident. Or its effects."

Rand narrowed his eyes. Effects? Except for the nausea, confusion and headaches in the first days after the explosion, Darnell didn't seem permanently damaged. Vanderhoven seemed to have a few additional issues. But were those due to the explosion? Or was he just enjoying being able to reduce cops and citizens alike to emotional wrecks with his chemicals? "What were the effects, Nurse Dumont?"

"I don't know."

"You didn't observe any of the effects?"

She looked around the room, confused. "I...I don't know."

"What about Ashley Kromm?" Echo asked.

Rand focused on Echo. He could see where she was going. Why hadn't he thought of that before? Because it was preposterous, that was why. Still...

Echo continued. "Was Ashley experiencing some of those effects during the time she spent with Wes Vanderhoven?"

The nurse's face reddened. "No. Ashley was fired because of…unfortunate behavior on her part."

Unfortunate. Rand would have to remember that one. "There was a lot of unfortunate behavior going on surrounding Wes Vanderhoven, wasn't there?"

The nurse pursed her lips. "I suppose."

"And what was the cause of that?"

"I'm sure I don't know."

"I'm not so sure."

"It wasn't any experimentation, if that's what you're thinking. I wouldn't have abided that." She glared at the doctor.

Right. Dumont was a regular saint. "Not unless you were better paid, at any rate."

The glare lifted to Rand.

"When did the 'unfortunate' things start happening?" he asked.

"Several days after the two arrived from Cranesbrook."

"And when did they stop?"

"When Wesley Vanderhoven left this

building." Nurse Dumont let out a heavy breath, her normally rigid posture sagging as if she couldn't hold out any longer. "He was causing those things, detective. The sex. And other things too. I have no idea how, but he was. He was like a kid playing practical jokes. Having his fun humiliating others."

"However he was doing it, he used his 'practical jokes,' as you call them, to kidnap a child. A baby girl. Do you know anything about that?"

"I'm sorry, I don't. He never brought a baby here."

Echo stood stoically in the corner, even though her heart had to be breaking all over again.

The need to touch her, to hold her, to promise everything would be okay pulled at him. But how could he make a promise he didn't know he could keep? A promise that might just end up hurting her more?

Frustration chomped at the back of Rand's neck like a damned rottweiler. Nobody seemed to understand anything about this accident, its effects, or what was going on with Wesley Vanderhoven. Least of all him. His only hope seemed to be sewing up the case against Morton and hoping additional search warrants for the doctor's home and finances would yield solid answers.

Rand brought his focus back to the nurse. Once he got her on record, he could get the arrest underway. "Did you keep Gage Darnell tied to his bed?"

"Twenty-four hours a day. Doctor's orders."

Morton slumped into his chair and buried his face in his hands.

Rand continued. "Did the doctor tell you why?"

"Dr. Morton said we had to keep Mr. Darnell from leaving the hospital."

"So you held him against his will and didn't inform his family."

"That's right."

That should be enough to get the warrants he needed. At least there was still a chance that he'd get some answers. But one last question hung in his mind. One detail that didn't add up. "If Darnell was tied to his bed twenty-four hours a day, how did he get away?"

"I don't know. He shouldn't have been able to." Nurse Dumont raised her chin. "No one let him go, that much I know. My nurses never cared for him unsupervised."

Another question unanswered. At least he could go to the source this time. Gage Darnell had some explaining to do.

Rand motioned to the cops in the doorway, then turned back to face Morton and Dumont. "These officers will write up a statement for you to sign, then they'll take you to the county jail and book you. The two of you are under arrest."

Morton groaned.

Dumont thrust out her chest. "I told you everything I know. You said you'd recommend—"

"You'll get your plea bargain. But first you can spend the night tasting a little of what you put Gage Darnell through."

Chapter Fourteen

Less than an hour's drive later, Rand and Echo strode up the front walk of the Sunrise Bed and Breakfast in Rehoboth Beach, Delaware. A three-story white house with a sprawling, columned veranda, the place was fully decked out with containers of flowers and rocking chairs inviting guests to step back into an infinitely more simple and easily understandable past.

Too bad that wasn't part of the afternoon's plan.

Rand led Echo inside. A brunette wearing what looked to be an expensive sweater headed them off in the foyer. "Welcome to Sunrise. Do you have a reservation?"

Despite her smile, Rand got the feeling she was not about to allow anyone past her without a damn good excuse. He pulled out his badge. "Detective McClellan with the Maryland State Police."

She stood a little straighter, as if worried he'd give her a ticket for slumping. "What can I help you with, Detective?"

"We need to speak to one of your guests. Gage Darnell."

"Yes. I believe he and his wife are in their room. I'll give him a buzz." The brunette scurried to the phone and punched in the call.

A moment later, the security expert Rand had once mistaken for a murderer appeared at the top of the grand staircase, his wife at his side. "McClellan? Echo? Come on up."

They followed the couple to a quaint room overlooking the water sparkling in the late-afternoon sun. The view rippled through old, wavy glass, as if it were a mirage too idyllic to be real.

Darnell and Lily sat on a love seat next

to a fireplace. Echo perched on the edge of a chair, and Rand stood behind her. There wasn't a chance he could sit. Not with the questions buzzing through his mind.

Darnell focused on Rand. "I assume you didn't drive up here for a leisurely chat. What did you find?"

Rand knew what he was afraid to hear. "We still haven't located Sloane."

"The baby?" Lily said.

Echo shook her head.

Darnell let out a heavy breath. "What is it, then?"

Rand searched his mind for a way to ask. Problem was, he wasn't sure what he was asking. "How did you escape Beech Grove?"

"I told you, I ran into the janitor and had to—"

Rand held up a hand to cut him off. "You were tied to the bed frame. How did you get your hands free?"

Darnell looked at his wife. He pressed his lips into a worried line.

The last thing Rand wanted was to field

lies from Darnell. Better to not give him the chance to tell any. "I know you didn't have any help from the clinic staff. I also know it's not possible for a man to get out of those restraints on his own."

Echo leaned forward in her chair. "Please. We need to know the truth. Strange things have been happening with Wesley Vanderhoven. We think he might be the one who took Zoe."

Darnell's complexion drained to white. "Vanderhoven? What strange things happened with Vanderhoven?"

"Not with him, actually. With the people around him." Echo glanced up at Rand, as if looking for help explaining the unexplainable.

As if he'd fare any better. "He seems to be able to amplify people's emotions."

Darnell's brows dipped low over dark eyes. "Amplify emotions?"

Rand nodded. "I first experienced it three days ago in Vanderhoven's room at Beech Grove. Fear. Grief. Depression."

"That's what you were asking about

when you came to see me at my office?" Darnell said.

"Yes. I thought it was all in my head. I'd feel an emotion, however slight, and suddenly it would take on a life of its own. It would grow so strong I had a hard time controlling it. Then it started happening to others. Echo, her babysitter, another cop."

"And you think Vanderhoven was causing this?"

Echo nodded. "We know he is. We just don't know how."

"What makes you think I have your answer?"

"You were in the explosion at Cranesbrook. Do you think Vanderhoven might have gotten access to some of the chemical from that explosion? Do you think that's what he's using to cause these emotional effects?"

Darnell looked down at Lily's hands covering his.

Lily tilted her head and gave him a troubled look, her blond hair swinging against her cheeks. "I don't think you have a choice, Gage."

So he did know something. Rand gripped the back of Echo's chair. "You have to tell me everything you know, Darnell. Is Vanderhoven using Project Cypress?"

Darnell raised his gaze to Rand's face. "No. Project Cypress doesn't cause emotional effects like you're talking about. At least I didn't feel them."

"What is it, then?" Echo asked. "What kind of chemical does Vanderhoven have?"

Darnell shook his head. "I don't think it's a chemical at all. And it's not Project Cypress. But if I'm right, it was caused by the chemicals in Project Cypress."

Rand had enough of these damn riddles. "Out with it, Darnell."

"I don't know how to explain." Darnell shook his head. The man was so pale, he looked as if he'd keel over. "After being exposed to those chemicals, I was able to do things. Things I could never do before. Things normal people can't do."

Rand was getting a headache, a throb of

frustration behind his right eye. "What things? What are you trying to say?"

Lily squeezed Darnell's fingers. "I think you're going to have to show them, Gage."

Darnell nodded.

Lily focused on Rand. "But you can't tell anyone, Detective. All right? No one. I don't want some agency deciding it would be beneficial to humanity to cut my husband open and study him like a lab rat."

A tremble lodged in Rand's gut. He didn't like the sound of that. He didn't like it at all. But he had to have the truth. Whatever it was, he needed to know. He nodded to Lily. "It's between us. You have my word."

Lily turned back to Darnell and gave him a supportive smile.

Darnell leaned back in the love seat. Focusing on the fireplace tools, he slipped into what looked like a deep concentration.

The fireplace poker clanked against the holder. It started to lift.

Rand blinked, but the vision didn't change.

The poker floated up into the air.

"You're moving that? With your mind?" He'd never have believed it without seeing it. He hardly believed it now.

Darnell kept his focus on the poker. "That's not all I can do. Watch."

The poker started to warp, to bend. It twisted into a pretzel shape, then slowly lowered to the fireplace's brick apron.

Darnell returned his gaze to Rand. "That's how I escaped Beech Grove. I didn't even know it was happening at first. I'd just think of getting those damn restraints off, and suddenly the things were unbuckled. Same with the locked door. When I reached the security fence in the forest, I finally figured out I could bend it, then bend it back so they wouldn't know I had gotten out."

Rand thought back to Darnell's appearance beside Rand's bed despite the fact that he always kept his doors locked. "That's how you got into my apartment."

"Yes."

"And the vase in Edmonston's office, the one that broke and distracted him."

Darnell nodded. "That was me."

Rand shook his head. "How? It seems impossible."

"Project Cypress. I don't know if that's what it was supposed to do to me. All I know is that's what it did. It gave me powers no normal man has. It gave me superpowers."

"And if that's the case," whispered Echo, "it might have given Wesley Vanderhoven superpowers of his own."

NEITHER RAND NOR ECHO said a word until his Crown Vic was speeding down the Lewes-Georgetown Highway on the way back to St. Stephens. The first words to pull Rand from his thoughts were a soft "Oh, God," from Echo's lips.

"My sentiments exactly."

"I guess we know for sure Vanderhoven is the one who took Zoe."

Rand nodded, his stomach tight. "I don't think superpowers are transferrable."

"The ability to amplify emotions. I can't believe it. It's like something out of a comic book."

It *was* unbelievable. But they'd seen the evidence. He could still picture that fireplace poker, hear the iron creak as it bent. Hell, with Vanderhoven, he'd *felt* the evidence, too. He'd been teetering on the edge of an emotional abyss since he'd first spoken to the lab tech.

"What about Bray?" Echo's voice faltered. "He was in that accident, too. Do you think he developed some kind of power?"

"Hard to tell." Rand glanced at Echo out of the corner of his eye. If her brother's fate was hard for her to accept before, this twist really complicated things. Now not only might Sloane be guilty of causing the explosion, he might be walking around with some sort of power himself.

And if he had a special mental ability like Darnell and Vanderhoven, why hadn't he used it to help himself out of this jam? Unless, of course, his power was invisibility.

Rand clutched the wheel with sweaty palms. Just this morning he would have laughed at that thought. Now it was all too real.

"And Zoe. If Vanderhoven has that effect on her…" Echo sucked in a harsh breath. The light from the setting sun glinted red off Echo's face, making the tears running down her cheeks look like blood.

Rand reached for her hand. Her fingers were cold and trembling.

Echo was right. Just the idea of poor baby Zoe in Vanderhoven's hands was hard to take. Especially since Rand didn't know how he'd save her. "Wait a second. Vanderhoven didn't have Zoe at Maritime Lullaby yesterday."

"No."

"So where was she?"

Echo's eyes burned into him. "She would have to be somewhere else. With someone else."

God, he hoped so. He hoped Vanderhoven wasn't stupid enough to leave a baby by herself. Not a worry he'd mention to Echo. "So who would he leave her with? He doesn't have any family. Not that we could locate, at any rate. And he said his only real friends work at Cranesbrook. The only one he named was Hank Riddell."

"Hank Riddell?"

"He's a research fellow there."

Echo's eyebrows tilted low. "The one who gave you that DVD of Bray?"

Rand nodded. "But I can't imagine him taking care of a baby. They have living quarters at Cranesbrook, but still…I can't see it."

Echo gasped, the sound coming from deep in her throat.

Again, his gut tensed. "You thought of someone?"

"Ashley Ashley Kromm. She thinks she's in love with him. And…"

"And what?"

"She got upset when I brought up Zoe's kidnapping. That's when she knocked my purse into the water."

Rand grabbed for his cell. A few seconds later he had Nick on the line. He explained the situation, leaving out mention of super-powers or anything else that would have

Nick sending him off to a place like Beech Grove wearing the latest in straitjacket fashion. "Ask Farrell to check out a woman named Ashley Kromm. I need addresses for her and everyone she knows. And I need cops at her home to recover Echo Sloane's baby, ASAP."

"Will do," Nick said over the phone.

"I'll be there as soon as I can."

"She mentioned a grandmother," Echo said.

"You hear that, Nick?"

"Got it."

Rand glanced at Echo. "Did she mention a name?"

"She didn't say."

"No name. Makes things harder. But maybe we can get phone records, DMV records, an apartment lease, something that will tell us who her grandmother is in case she has a different last name. I'll call you back when we get closer to St. Stephens, Nick."

He hung up and focused his full attention on the road ahead, pushing the car to go as fast as he dared. If they were lucky at all, Ashley or her grandmother would be alone with the baby. He could get Zoe and Echo to safety and deal with figuring out how to stop Vanderhoven another time.

After Echo and her baby were safe.

Problem was, luck hadn't been his friend lately.

He shifted in his seat. If Vanderhoven was there, nothing could stop him from taking Echo, too. Nothing could stop him from manipulating her emotions, bending her to his will…even destroying her.

Rand's gut tightened like a fist.

If he took Echo with him, he'd be putting her in danger. God knew he couldn't protect her. He'd already failed.

He glanced at her. She'd wiped her tears, and her eyes now shone with determination. The blond strands of her hair glowed like flame.

She'd hate him for not taking her, but it couldn't be helped. Maybe it was even for the best. If she hated him, he couldn't hurt her. He couldn't let her down. He couldn't lose her. Because he knew if Echo died because of him, he would never forgive himself.

He wouldn't even want to live.

Chapter Fifteen

Echo's pulse drummed in her ears. She watched the quiet streets of St. Stephens scroll by outside the car windows, but all she could wrap her mind around was that the miles of pavement were bringing her closer to Zoe.

And the time ticking away.

Rand hadn't said much since his call to his supervisor, and Echo hadn't pushed it. He'd talked on the phone a couple of times, but when he'd admitted they hadn't found Zoe yet, she'd let it go. She'd wanted him to concentrate. She'd wanted him focused on getting to St. Stephens as soon as possible. Focused on finding her Zoe.

But she couldn't hold it in any longer.

Now that they'd arrived in St. Stephens, she needed to know. "They would tell you if they found her, wouldn't they? I mean, if she was at Ashley's house, they'd let you know, right?"

Shadows of falling twilight cupped his cheekbones. The glow of his dash lit the hard planes of his forehead and long straight nose. "They'd let me know if they found anything."

So they hadn't.

She wrapped her arms around her middle, trying to stem the tremble that shook her. This waiting was impossible. She couldn't take much more.

The slowing of the car jolted her out of her thoughts. She peered out the window at the squat little building that housed the St. Stephens PD. "If they haven't found anything, why are we stopping here?"

Rand gripped the wheel and stared straight ahead.

Panic surged around the edges of her mind. There was something he didn't want to tell her. Something he was holding back.

The warning of tears knifed through her sinuses and burned at the back of her eyes. "Is it Zoe? Did something happen? Is she okay?"

"I don't know. Like I said, we haven't found her yet."

"Then what is it? Why are we here? What don't you want to tell me?"

He pulled in a deep breath and pivoted toward her. "I'm not taking you with me, Echo. You need to stay here."

She couldn't have heard him right. "What?"

"It's too dangerous. Vanderhoven might be there."

"Zoe might be there!"

"I can get her. I can bring her back to you."

He couldn't be saying these things. He knew she wanted to be there. He knew she *had* to be. "You can't be serious. You can't expect me to sit here and wait."

"I have to make sure you're safe. This is the only way."

"I don't care if I'm safe. What's safety worth if something happens to my baby?

What's safety worth if I can't be there for her?" Tears flooded her eyes, turning Rand's face and the dark interior of the car into a blur. "You can't do this to me."

"I'm sorry, Echo."

She shook her head. Her hair whipped against her cheeks and stuck to the tracks of her tears. "You're not sorry. Don't lie."

"I am. If I could protect you another way, I would."

"I don't want your protection. Can't you understand that? I want to help you find Zoe. I want my baby back."

"I can get her back. But if you get hurt or killed or God knows what..." His fingers dug into her arm. He turned her to face him. "I can't be the one responsible."

That was it. He couldn't handle the guilt...like the guilt he'd felt at his father's suicide. The feeling of responsibility that had haunted him since. "If something happens to me, you don't have to feel guilty. This is my decision. Not yours. I'll except the responsibility. I'll accept the risk. It's worth it to me."

"It doesn't work that way, Echo."

"Why not? Why can't I have a say over my own life? Why can't I be there for my own child?"

"I would be bringing a civilian into a situation I know is dangerous. I can't do that."

"Don't pretend this is about police procedure. This has nothing to do with rules."

His gaze dropped to his hands on her arms. "You're right. It doesn't." He relaxed his fingers, letting her go.

She gasped in a breath and held it, waiting for the rest.

"If something happened to you, I couldn't..." His eyes burned into hers. Lines of regret bracketed his mouth and spanned his forehead. "I can't let it happen."

A sob racked her body. She fought it back. "You're protecting yourself, you know. Not me."

He turned away from her, staring through the windshield once again.

She was right. She knew it. "You don't want to feel guilty if I get hurt."

He raked his hair from his forehead and

let out a long breath. "No, Echo. I don't want to lose you." His voice ached with feeling, with pain.

A shiver spread over her. A tremble shaking her to her toes.

"Please trust me, Echo. This once, please trust me to do what's best for you. For Zoe."

Could she? She didn't know.

A distorted voice barked from Rand's radio. A name, Molly Bakerhof.

Rand turned off the radio and laid his hand on hers, his skin rough and warm. "We'll talk. When I get back with Zoe. We'll take our time and sort everything out."

Echo pulled in a shaky breath. He wanted her to get out of the car. He wanted her to just give up and walk away. Let him handle everything.

Something she couldn't do.

She pulled her hand out from under his. Taking a deep breath, she raised her chin. "I can get out of the car, Rand, if you insist. But I can't trust you. After this I'll never trust you again." She threw open the passenger door, stepped out onto the curb and vowed to figure out why the name Molly Bakerhof seemed so familiar.

Chapter Sixteen

Rand bracketed his radio mike and focused on finding the house belonging to Molly Bakerhof. Now that they'd located Ashley's maternal grandmother, it was only a matter of time before he had Zoe back in Echo's arms.

Provided the baby was there.

Provided nothing went wrong.

He hadn't told Echo all his fears. Even if he did find Zoe, even if he could put her whole and healthy back into her mother's arms, there was no guarantee Vanderhoven would give up there. He clearly wanted Sloane. And until Echo's brother showed his face, Echo and Zoe were in danger. They were tools at Vanderhoven's disposal.

He would have to get them out of the area, hide them far away.

He shook his head. No chance of that. Echo would never leave. Not with her brother out there. She would want to help him, save him herself. Even if it meant she was putting herself smack in Vanderhoven's sights.

She would never trust Rand to find Bray.

With thoughts of Echo came a fresh wave of pain. When he'd told her he was afraid of losing her, he'd meant it. He didn't know how he'd come to feel so much for her so quickly, but he had. His chest ached whenever he looked at her. Whenever he smelled her scent and heard her voice, he could feel something shift inside him that would never shift back.

And the prospect of losing her trust was only slightly less disturbing than the thought of her losing her life.

He gripped the wheel, palms slick with sweat. He couldn't think of Echo now. He had to focus on getting Zoe, delivering her safely into her mother's arms.

Molly Bakerhof lived in a four-unit that looked as if it was built by the same architects that designed government buildings in the sixties. Blocklike and constructed of smooth, beige brick, the building had only one front and one back entrance and windows so small the landlord had to have offered bribes to get it past the fire inspector.

Two brown and beige state trooper cars pulled to the curb just before he did. He climbed out and joined the troopers. "One of you take the front entrance, one the back. I'll go to the apartment door. Don't let anyone in."

A trooper named Smith gave him a confused look. "This it? Just the three of us?"

"Three is plenty." If only Ashley and her grandmother were inside. If Vanderhoven was there, an entire SWAT team wouldn't be enough. But something told him he couldn't wait for more backup to arrive. He didn't even know if more was on the way. And he didn't have a second to waste. "Let's go."

The troopers took their positions. Rand mounted the stairs to Molly Bakerhof's unit on the second floor, his footsteps hollow on the wood stairs. At the door, he paused to listen for voices. A baby's cry drifted under the apartment door.

Zoe.

Taking a deep breath, he rapped on the door with his knuckles. "Mrs. Bakerhof? This is the Maryland State Police. Please open the door."

A scurry of footsteps sounded inside.

They couldn't get out. Thanks to the small windows and the troopers stationed below, Ashley and her grandmother weren't going anywhere. But he wasn't going to wait at the door politely and let them try something stupid, either. "Open the door, or I will."

The knob rattled and the door swung inward. A woman with blue eyes and the creased and weathered face of a sailor peered out. "Please, come in, Officer. What on earth is this about?"

He stepped inside. Pulse thrumming in his

ears, he scanned the plain living room, sizing up corners and potential blind spots where Vanderhoven could be hiding. The gold draperies from the seventies. The brown couch that could be brand-new, if it weren't so out of date. The tiny galley kitchen.

The lab tech wasn't there. At least not in the apartment's main rooms. There was little sign of Zoe either.

Rand turned back to the old woman. "Do you have a baby in this apartment, Mrs. Bakerhof?"

"A baby? Yes. I'm taking care of a baby as a favor to her mother."

"Who is her mother?"

"She's a patient at the Beech Grove Clinic. She's very ill." She waved her hand about her head. "Mental problems. Why are you asking about the baby?"

Rand ignored the question. "Where *is* the baby?"

"In the bedroom. She's just had her bath and now it's her bedtime."

"Is there anyone else with you in this apartment?"

"Why, yes. My granddaughter."

"Ashley Kromm?"

"Yes."

"Where is she?"

"In the bedroom taking care of the baby, of course."

Rand was afraid of that. He pushed past the woman.

She scampered after Rand as he turned down the short hall. "Why are you concerned about the baby? Nothing has happened to her mother, has it?"

"No." He reached the bedroom door. Preparing himself for anything, he pushed it open.

The blond nurse from Beech Grove stood next to a double bed, propping Zoe on her hip with one arm. In her free hand she held a cordless telephone to her ear.

"Put the phone down, Ashley."

Ashley lowered the phone and dropped it on the white woven bedspread.

Rand stepped toward her. Slowly. Steadily. "Who were you talking to?"

Ashley shook her head.

She didn't have to answer. He already knew. "It was Vanderhoven, wasn't it?"

Ashley stared at him defiantly. "Wes didn't do anything wrong."

"Hand me the baby, Ashley."

Again, the young nurse shook her head. "The baby's mother is sick. She couldn't take care of her."

"The baby's mother is Echo Sloane. You know that."

Zoe's little brow crumpled. She shoved a thumb in her mouth and grabbed a fistful of her own hair in her free hand.

"No. This isn't the same baby. It can't be. Wes wouldn't do that. He wouldn't take a child from her mother. Not unless the mother couldn't take care of her. It happened the way he said."

Rand kept approaching, step after step. "It's over, Ashley. Everything is going to be okay."

Tears welled up in her eyes and ran down her cheeks. "You can't hurt him. He's brilliant. Really. You can't put him in prison."

"We'll sort it out. Everything will be okay. You'll see. Now I need you to hand me the baby." He extended his arms toward her and opened his palms.

Ashley's lower lip trembled.

"It's okay." The poor girl was so mixed up, he wasn't sure what she'd do. Love did that. It turned everything on its head. Changed priorities. Changed lives. For better and for worse.

"Everything is okay. Just hand me the baby." Rand's fingertips touched a ruffle on Zoe's little pink pajamas. An inch more, and he'd have control.

"Don't listen to him, Ashley." The words came from behind Rand, the voice unmistakable.

Wes Vanderhoven.

A wave of desperation crashed over Rand, followed by another. He lunged forward, grabbing Zoe from Ashley's arms, cradling her little body to his chest.

He had to save the baby. He couldn't let Vanderhoven win. He'd promised Echo he'd bring the baby back, and that was what he was going to do. No matter what it took, he wouldn't fail this time.

ECHO THREADED HER BODY between the last box of lighthouse lamps and a new shipment of children's clothing. Fighting through the clutter, she reached the small desk, computer and file cabinets that formed Maritime Lullaby's office. She knelt in front of the small gray safe. Her fingers trembled as she turned the dial, reciting the combination in her head. She had to try twice before she remembered the sequence she'd used nearly every working day. The lock released with a click. She pulled the door open.

Manila envelopes jammed with cash, credit receipts and personal checks stuffed the safe, waiting for Joyce's regular Monday bank drop. Echo pulled out one envelope, then another, finally locating yesterday's deposit.

Echo knew she'd remembered the name Molly Bakerhof when she'd heard it come over Rand's radio. But it had taken precious minutes to figure out why. And precious more to figure out how to slip out of the police station without being noticed.

A woman by that name had come into the store just yesterday, when Echo was helping Joyce. Echo could still picture her kind, creased face and twinkling blue eyes. She'd purchased a stuffed orange crab, a soft baby blanket and a little pair of pink jammies covered with white shells. Things for a baby. Things for Zoe.

And she'd paid with a personal check.

Vanderhoven must have known Ashley's grandmother was shopping in St. Stephens. He must have figured out she would come to Maritime Lullaby to purchase baby things. He'd come to find Molly Bakerhof, not Echo. He'd missed the older woman by minutes.

Echo found the envelope dated yesterday. Bending the fastener open, she dumped the contents on the desk. She shoved the cash and credit slips to the side and picked up the stack of checks. She flipped through them. Her fingers couldn't move fast enough.

They slipped on the paper. But finally she found a check bearing ocean scenes and written in an older woman's precise hand. Echo memorized the apartment address and raced for the door.

She had to save her little girl.

Chapter Seventeen

Rand held Zoe tight to his chest. His pulse thundered in his ears. His hands shook. He couldn't let Vanderhoven take Echo's baby. He would die first.

Zoe shrieked. Her breath caught, leaving her mouth open and arms flailing in a soundless scream.

Fear for the little girl swelled in him until he could hardly think, fueled nearly past reason by Vanderhoven's power. She was so upset, so frightened. He had to get her out of here.

He moved his right hand to his holster. He unsnapped his weapon and lifted it free.

"No!" Ashley lunged at him, fingers bared like claws. She hit him, scratched at his face.

Pain sliced his cheek, but he hardly felt it. All he could think of was Zoe. Of the fear swamping him, pulling him down. He couldn't let her go. He had to get her out of here. He couldn't let Vanderhoven hurt her.

He turned his back to Ashley, using his shoulders to shield himself, to shield the baby.

She threw herself at him again, ripping at his arm, his gun hand.

He jabbed back at her with his elbow. He felt it connect.

She grunted and fell backward. Her angry screams turned to sobs.

"Put the gun down, McClellan." Vanderhoven stared at him, those eyes burning and chilling at the same time. Those eyes…

He had to take the monster out. He had to stop him from all he was doing, all he would do. He raised the gun. Gritting his teeth, he lined up the sights on Vanderhoven's smug face.

"I said put it down." Vanderhoven's stare sharpened, penetrating like a pale-blue laser.

Rand's hand began to tremble. The Glock's barrel dipped and bobbed. The sights swung wildly.

He couldn't keep control. He couldn't remain steady.

"You'll hurt the baby with that gun, McClellan. You'll kill her. And it will all be your fault."

Rand's palm were slick with sweat. The more he tried to hold it, the more the weapon's grip slid. It bobbed one last time and fell from his hand, clattering onto the hardwood floor.

He'd lost all control of the situation, if he'd ever had it. He had to get the hell out.

He stumbled through the bedroom door. Zoe screamed, squirming against his shoulder, flailing her tiny fists in the air.

He had to get her to safety. Away from Vanderhoven and his damn power. He didn't know what the hell had happened to the troopers below, but if he could find them, maybe the three of them could hold Vanderhoven. Maybe they had a chance.

Ashley's keening cries followed him

from the room. In the hall, he nearly ran into her grandmother.

The woman leaned on the wall, as if she couldn't stand on her own. Sweat beaded her upper lip. Tears streamed down her lined cheeks. She gripped her chest with one hand, in pain. "Ashley!"

Rand forced his feet to move past her, to keep carrying him down the hall. She could be having a heart attack, but he couldn't do anything about it. He couldn't help her. Not now. He had to focus on getting Zoe out before the roar of emotion in his ears overpowered everything. Before it dragged them both under.

He reached the apartment door. Grabbing the knob, he ripped the door open and stumbled onto the stair landing. He gripped the railing with his free hand. Legs shaking so badly it was all he could do to stand, he started descending the stairs.

Vanderhoven was behind him. He could feel it in the panic surging in his blood, taste it in the tinny dryness of his mouth.

Angry voices rose from the neighboring

apartment. The door flew open and a woman stared down at him. A man spilled out of the apartment behind her, a shout still on his lips. "I saw the way you looked at him," he yelled at her. Then his squinty green eyes focused on Rand. In his hand he held a gun.

Rand tried to speed up, tried to hurry down the stairs. He could hardly control his body. He could hardly control his thoughts.

"That's him, isn't it?" the gunman bellowed at the woman. "You have another one."

Rand stumbled on the steps. He slid down on one hip, holding Zoe high on his shoulder, protecting her from the fall.

The man raised the gun, pointing it at Rand.

"What do you think you're doing?" the woman screamed. "Do you think you can kill every man who looks at me?"

Rand turned his back to the man, trying to protect the baby. He braced himself for the crack of gunfire, for the impact of the bullet.

The gun exploded, reverberating through the stairwell.

Zoe screamed. But the thud of the bullet never came.

Rand looked down into the baby's face, checked her thrashing pink-clad limbs. She was all right. Frightened, but fine. The bullet must have gone wide.

He gasped in a breath, trying to tamp down his panic, trying to think. Grasping the railing, he pulled himself to his feet and looked over his shoulder.

The woman sprawled on the landing, red staining her chest. A sob broke from her shooter's lips, and he let the gun drop from his hand.

"Call 911." Rand spit the words from his parched throat.

"Do you really think the authorities can help, McClellan?" Vanderhoven's skeletal frame loomed on the landing above. "You're the authorities, and you don't seem to be doing a very good job."

The shooter collapsed in a fit of sobs. He

threw himself over the woman, unable to function, unable to help.

Ignoring the couple, Vanderhoven thunked slowly down the steps toward Rand like doom closing in. He stared with those eyes, his gaze drilling into Rand, pummeling him until he couldn't move, could hardly think.

Despair swamped him. He couldn't get away. He couldn't save Zoe. He couldn't keep her from getting hurt. He had failed again. Utterly failed.

Vanderhoven stepped over Rand and stopped on the step below. Bending down, he reached for Zoe and took her from Rand's useless, trembling arms.

The apartment building entrance flew open. "You stay away from my baby."

Her voice soared over the swirling rumble in Rand's head. He focused on it, grasped hold of it like a lifeline.

He could hear Vanderhoven walk down the rest of the steps. He could hear Echo's scream of fury. He could hear her fight. But he couldn't *do* anything about it. He couldn't stop Vanderhoven. He couldn't help Echo and Zoe. He couldn't even push himself off these damn stairs.

The door slammed shut.

Quiet settled over him, broken only by the man's sobs drifting down from the second-floor landing. Slowly the storm of emotion ebbed. Too slowly. He couldn't wait.

Rand struggled to his feet. He forced his mind to function. The woman needed help. She was shot. She could be dying. But if he raced up to help her, Vanderhoven would get away. He'd take Echo and Zoe. He'd hurt them. Or worse. "Is she alive?"

The man looked up, his face streaked with tears. Choking on a sob, he nodded. "There's so much blood."

"Apply pressure to the wound to stop the bleeding."

Ashley peeked out her apartment door. "My grandmother—"

"Call 911. Right now."

She disappeared back into the apartment. Rand forced his legs to stop shaking, to hold his weight. Negotiating the rest of the stairs, he pushed his way outside.

Vanderhoven held Zoe in one arm, blocking a desperate Echo with the other. He pulled them toward one of the state trooper's cars. Echo grabbed at him, thrashing, fighting all the way. Slowing him down despite the emotion that had to be ripping her apart.

Vanderhoven glanced back in his direction.

Another gush of emotion shook Rand, this time so strong he couldn't sort one feeling from another. He bit down on his lip, using the pain to hold on to sanity for as long as he could. The taste of blood filled his mouth.

A groan came from the side of the apartment entrance. He looked down, spotting a brown shirt between the boxwood hedge and the beige brick. The trooper held his head in his hands, clearly distraught.

His gun.

Rand slipped behind the hedge. Reaching along the trooper's side, he located his holster and pulled his weapon free. Fitting the gun into his hand, he started after Vanderhoven.

The lab tech had the car door open. Still holding Zoe, he was trying to push Echo inside, as if he'd given up breaking free of her and decided to take her along.

Echo held his arm. Lashing out, she nailed Vanderhoven's shin with a sharp kick.

Rand pushed his feet to move faster across the rough front lawn. He held the gun in front of him. He had no idea if a weapon would do him any good this time. His sure hadn't before. But at least it gave him a fighting chance.

A chance to save the woman he loved.

The woman he loved. He loved Echo Sloane.

Emotion slammed through him, but this time it was different. Not muddy and confused and debilitating, but clear as fresh air. He loved Echo. He hadn't realized it until now, but it was true.

The swirl of feeling honed to a point, a point centering on Echo. His vision narrowed, blocking out the neighborhood. Blocking out the street. Even blocking out Vanderhoven. It sharpened and brightened like a star in a dark sky.

The roar in his ears lessened, then died. The writhing sensation in his chest slowly faded. Until all that was left was Echo. All that was left was her.

Wait.

Vanderhoven hadn't stopped using his powers. Rand could hear the trooper still groaning from the bushes. Echo's screams still pierced the air. Nothing had changed.

Except him. He had broken free.

How could that be true? Unless…

There was one other time…when Zoe was kidnapped. Vanderhoven's powers hadn't affected Echo then. They had worked on everyone, but not her. Not her because Echo had blocked them with the strength of her love. Her love for Zoe.

Just like he was blocking them now.

Vanderhoven turned to him as he reached the car. He glanced at the gun in

Rand's hand with as much concern as he would give a squirt gun. "This again, McClellan? Drop it. You don't want to fire that thing and hit your girlfriend, do you? Or the baby." He let go of Echo and grabbed Zoe from the car seat, holding her in front of him like a shield.

The baby thrashed in his hands, her face red, her voice hoarse from screaming.

A wave of doubt swept over Rand. Maybe this wasn't the right thing. Maybe he was risking too much. Maybe Vanderhoven was right...

No.

He focused on Echo. His love for her was strong, but not strong enough to fight off Vanderhoven's power. At least not alone. "Echo, you have to listen to me. You have to hear me."

Echo clawed at Vanderhoven, trying to rip Zoe from his grasp. A growl of fury rose from her throat.

"Echo," Rand said. He had to make her listen. He could feel Vanderhoven's power battering against him, trying to sweep him away. "I love you, Echo. More than I've ever loved anyone."

She glanced at him for a split second. Her lips pulled back from her teeth in an expression of pain.

"You were right," Rand told her. "I was trying to protect myself. I knew you would sacrifice everything for Zoe. Everything. And I couldn't face losing you."

Tears blurred his vision and streamed down his face. He let them come. He let emotion sweep over him. His love for Echo. His need to make things right with her. To tell her how he felt. It was all that mattered. "It never occurred to me that is exactly what I love about you. Your devotion to Zoe. Your devotion to your brother. You never run. You never withdraw. You fight for what you want. You fight for those you love."

He could feel her eyes focus on him more than see them. As if her love reached out and joined with his. And as their feelings twined together, they formed an unbreakable bond.

"I love you, Rand." Her voice was little more than a whisper, but to him it sounded like a shout.

Rand raised the Glock. Even with Vanderhoven holding the baby, he could get a clear shot. He lined up his sights on the bastard's head, his hands steady. "Put the baby down, Vanderhoven. This is over."

"Not so fast." Vanderhoven pulled Rand's gun from his waistband. He started bringing the barrel to the baby's head.

Pop. Pop. Pop. Gunfire cracked through the neighborhood as Rand pumped three rounds into the lab tech.

Vanderhoven slumped against the car. The gun fell from his hand.

Echo grabbed Zoe and cradled the baby safely to her chest as Vanderhoven slid to the ground.

Chapter Eighteen

Rand watched Echo lower Zoe into her crib and pull the soft white blanket to the baby's chest, leaving her hands free. Zoe plugged her thumb in her mouth and grasped her wispy brown curls in her other fist.

She'd been through an emotional hell, but she seemed to have recovered just fine. Much more quickly than Rand had. He still felt shaky, still unsure. At least about everything except his feelings for Echo and her child. "She looks content."

Echo nodded. "She looks sleepy. Screaming like a banshee will take it out of you. Just ask me. I know." She glanced up at him, her lips curving into a beautiful smile.

His chest ached at the thought of all they'd

been through. And not just them. At least no one had been killed. Even Ashley's grandmother and the woman whose husband had shot her were expected to recover.

Maxie Wallace wasn't so lucky. And Officer Lance Woodard. Rand might not ever be able to prove Vanderhoven's superpowers caused Woodard's death, but he knew it was true. And although Vanderhoven's death wouldn't bring the two St. Stephens officers back, any more than Edmonston's death brought back Richard, at least he knew that justice was served.

He pushed all that out of his mind and focused on Echo. She'd changed from her torn and dirty clothes into a soft silk skirt and blouse, and looking at her now, he couldn't imagine not touching her.

He ran a hand down her arm and took her hand in his. "You were amazing today."

"What? You liked my screams?"

"You might have been screaming, but you never gave up."

She looked down at her daughter. "I had Zoe to keep me going."

He nodded. Just like the day the baby had been kidnapped, Echo had kept herself together by focusing on her baby. By loving her child.

She looked up at him. "You didn't do so badly, either."

He shook his head. "That's not true. I folded. At least until you got there. Then I had you to keep me going." He felt so much for her, his chest ached with it. But unlike the artificially strong emotion Vanderhoven had caused, the ache was clear and clean and sure.

He loved Echo Sloane. More than he knew he could love anyone, especially in so short a time. He wanted to be with her, to forge a future together. A future that was strong and bright and full of love. A future he could focus on full-time in the doubtless weeks he'd be on administrative leave. His shrink would be proud.

But first… "We need to talk."

She nodded. Slipping her hand into his, she led him out of the room, leaving Zoe to sleep. When they reached the living room, she turned to face him. "What do you want to talk about?"

"Your brother."

She pursed her lips and waited for him to continue.

"I don't want him to come between us."

"I'm not going to accept that he's guilty of causing that explosion, Rand. I can't."

"I know." Since the mess with Vanderhoven had ended, he'd been searching for a reason Sloane might have sabotaged Project Cypress, a reason Echo might accept. He might not know as much about Echo's brother as she did, but he did know the former Special Ops soldier had likely witnessed the dark side of war in Afghanistan, and that type of experience never left a man unscathed. "What if your brother objected to Project Cypress on a moral level? I'm sure he saw things in Afghanistan. Horrible things. What if he didn't want this new chemical weapon to be used? What if that was his reason?"

Echo shook her head. "Bray lived through some rough things in Afghanistan. Things that changed him. Things he would never talk about. But he loves his country. He might demonstrate against something he thought was morally wrong. He might try to bring it to people's attention, try to get it changed. But he wouldn't sabotage it, especially if it meant hurting other people. That's just not Bray."

Rand let out a long breath. Clearly she wouldn't accept any kind of explanation. "I love you, Echo. More than I can say. When I told you I didn't want to lose you, I meant it. Not to Vanderhoven. And not to a disagreement over your brother."

"I can't pretend to believe something I never will."

He threaded his fingers with hers. Her skin was so soft, so tender. Yet underneath she was stronger than steel. "What if we agree to disagree about Bray?"

She tilted her head in an unspoken question.

"What if I promise to do whatever I can to clear his name?"

She nodded. "And what do you want from me?"

"If the evidence proves him guilty, you have to promise to understand when I have to do my job."

She nodded. "Okay."

He gathered her in his arms and lowered his lips to hers. She was soft and sweet. Everything he could ever want. Everything he never dared dream he could have. Love swept over him, pervasive and insane. A different kind of insanity. One that brought strength instead of weakness. Peace instead of guilt. And while control wasn't remotely part of the mix, it was an out-of-control feeling he could more than live with.

An out-of-control feeling he wanted to get lost in.

He pulled back just enough to look into her eyes. "I want you, Echo. I want to touch you and kiss you and know you. I know this is happening fast. But I have to know if you want me, too."

"Yeah. I want you. It is happening fast. But I wouldn't have it any other way."

Warmth radiated through him. The calm after the storm. Heaven after purgatory. "At least we've already seen each other at our worst. That's something."

Her lips curved into a smile. "And at our best."

"No, that's still to come." He gathered her into his arms and kissed her. Emotion surged through him, hot and urgent and on the edge of control.

Echo slipped her arm around him. Pulling the tail of his shirt free, she ran her fingertips over his bare skin.

Goosebumps rose, spreading up his sides and over his back. Heat built inside him. Passion, yet so much more. A press of emotion he'd never let himself feel before. He wanted to let himself go, to fall over the edge with Echo in his arms.

He grasped her hand, backpedaling into

the hall. She went along willingly, eagerly. As if she was in as much of a hurry as he.

The door to her bedroom stood open. Rand pulled Echo inside. Closing the door behind them, he took her back in his arms.

Her breasts pressed softly against his chest. She looked up at him, hunger in her eyes.

A reflection of his own. He wanted her more than he could say, more than he could even understand. And although the thought of drowning in his feelings for her still scared the hell out of him, he wasn't about to pull back. Not ever again. He was done with pulling back where Echo was concerned.

He slipped his fingers through her hair, the silken strands winding and tangling as he cradled her head in his palm. Lowering his mouth, he crushed his lips to hers and teased his tongue inside.

She opened, taking him, challenging him to give her more. She hooked her leg around his, pulling his groin against her. A low moan rose in her throat.

The sexiest sound he'd ever heard.

He smoothed his hand down her body and over the soft fabric of her skirt and the firm flesh beneath. He wanted to feel her skin. He kissed her neck, moving down over her collarbone. He nuzzled lower, into the cleavage between impossibly full, ripe breasts.

Pressure built inside him, as if all the passion he'd ever known demanded release. "I want you naked. I need to see you. I need…"

She worked her hands between them and grasped her blouse. She fumbled with the buttons, half tearing the blouse open. She unfastened the center clasp on her bra. Arching her back, she pulled the cups apart.

Her breasts were more full and luscious than he'd even imagined, large areolas dark against white skin. Her nipples were peaked and excited and hard.

Hunger rose in him, hunger he couldn't

control. "You are so beautiful." He took her nipples into his mouth, devouring first one breast and then the other. She tasted sweet, impossibly sweet. Like he could suckle her forever and never get his fill.

Pressure built in his groin. Need throbbed.

She rubbed her body against him, her belly and skirt soft against his fly.

He wanted to be free of these damn pants. He wanted to be inside her.

"I need more. I need all of you," he said in a moan. He gathered the soft skirt in his hands, pulling the fabric up her thighs, over her buttocks. He pushed her panties down and let them fall to the floor. Once she was bare, he slipped his hand into the heat and wetness between her legs.

She made a sound deep in her throat. Spreading wide, she moved against him.

He could smell her, light and sweet and so erotic. His erection bucked to be free. He felt as if he would explode, as if he couldn't hold back.

"I want you." Echo's voice was rough, guttural.

He nearly ripped the button off his pants and lowered his fly. He shoved his pants down his legs. He was hard and ready, his tip reaching for her before he'd slipped on the condom.

Her hands found him, helping him sheath himself. Each stroke of her fingers ripped along his nerves. Each touch drove him past insanity.

He lifted her, pressing her back against the closed door, positioning himself between her legs.

Gripping his shoulders, she embraced his waist with her thighs and lowered herself.

He slid deep inside.

Her wet heat surrounded him. Her scent engulfed him. He looked into her face— that tender, angelic face—and all he could see was the inferno in her eyes.

He thrust into her. Hard. Deep. His breath roared in his ears. Sweat broke over his skin and trickled down his back, down his chest. The heat between them built, melting them, joining them, as if he'd never been joined with anyone before.

A cry broke from her lips. A scream raw with passion. Her muscles gripped him, pulling him in, urging him on, pulling him with her over the edge.

He crested and broke, his voice joining hers. And as he spilled into her, he knew he would never be the same.

* * * * *

Don't miss next month's exciting conclusion of the SECURITY BREACH *miniseries with* TRIGGERED RESPONSE *by Patricia Rosemoor, only in Harlequin Intrigue!*

New York Times *bestselling author
Linda Lael Miller is back with a new
romance featuring the heartwarming
McKettrick family from
Silhouette Special Edition.*

SIERRA'S HOMECOMING
by Linda Lael Miller

*On sale December 2006,
wherever books are sold.*

Turn the page for a sneak preview!

Soft, smoky music poured into the room.

The next thing she knew, Sierra was in Travis's arms, close against that chest she'd admired earlier, and they were slow dancing.

Why didn't she pull away?

"Relax," he said. His breath was warm in her hair.

She giggled, more nervous than amused. What was the matter with her? She was attracted to Travis, had been from the first, and he was clearly attracted to her. They were both adults. Why not enjoy a little slow dancing in a ranch-house kitchen?

Because slow dancing led to other things. She took a step back and felt the counter flush against her lower back. Travis naturally came with her, since they were holding hands and he had one arm around her waist.

Simple physics.

Then he kissed her.

Physics again—this time, not so simple.

"Yikes," she said, when their mouths parted.

He grinned. "Nobody's ever said that after I kissed them."

She felt the heat and substance of his body pressed against hers. "It's going to happen, isn't it?" she heard herself whisper.

"Yep," Travis answered.

"But not tonight," Sierra said on a sigh.

"Probably not," Travis agreed.

"When, then?"

He chuckled, gave her a slow, nibbling kiss. "Tomorrow morning," he said. "After you drop Liam off at school."

"Isn't that…a little…soon?"

"Not soon enough," Travis answered, his voice husky. "Not nearly soon enough."

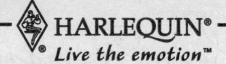

HARLEQUIN®
Live the emotion™

American **ROMANCE**®
Heart, Home & Happiness

◆ HARLEQUIN®
Blaze™
Red-hot reads.

Harlequin® Historical
Historical Romantic Adventure!

◆ HARLEQUIN®
HARLEQUIN ROMANCE®
From the Heart, For the Heart

◆ HARLEQUIN®
INTRIGUE
Breathtaking Romantic Suspense

Medical Romance™...
love is just a heartbeat away

N**ext**™
**There's the life you planned.
And there's what comes next.**

◆ HARLEQUIN®
Presents~
Seduction and Passion Guaranteed!

◆ HARLEQUIN®
Super Romance®
Exciting, Emotional, Unexpected

HARLEQUIN®

Super Romance®

...there's more to the story!

Superromance.
A *big* satisfying read about unforgettable
characters. Each month we offer *six* very different
stories that range from family drama to adventure
and mystery, from highly emotional stories to
romantic comedies—and much more! Stories
about people you'll believe in and care about.
Stories too compelling to put down....

Our authors are among today's *best* romance
writers. You'll find familiar names and talented
newcomers. Many of them are award winners—
and you'll see why!

If you want the biggest and best
in romance fiction, you'll get it
from Superromance!

Exciting, Emotional, Unexpected...

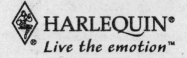

HARLEQUIN®
Live the emotion™

HARLEQUIN®
Presents

**The world's bestselling romance series...
The series that brings you your favorite authors,
month after month:**

Helen Bianchin...Emma Darcy
Lynne Graham...Penny Jordan
Miranda Lee...Sandra Marton
Anne Mather...Carole Mortimer
Susan Napier...Michelle Reid

and many more uniquely talented authors!

Wealthy, powerful, gorgeous men...
Women who have feelings just like your own...
The stories you love, set in exotic, glamorous locations...

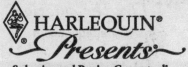

HARLEQUIN®
Presents

Seduction and Passion Guaranteed!

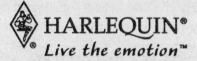

Harlequin® Historical
Historical Romantic Adventure!

Imagine a time of chivalrous knights and unconventional ladies, roguish rakes and impetuous heiresses, rugged cowboys and spirited frontierswomen— these rich and vivid tales will capture your imagination!

Harlequin Historical . . . they're too good to miss!

HHDIR06